In Dogs We Trust

In Dogs We Trust

Sharon Henegar

Saturday Books

Published by Saturday Books
PO Box 4592
Salem, OR 97302

ISBN 978-0-9840648-7-8
Library of Congress Control Number: 2011908579
Henegar, Sharon L.
In dogs we trust / Sharon L. Henegar
McGuire, Louisa (Fictitious Character)—Fiction
Counterfeiting—Fiction
Inns—Fiction
Humorous Fiction
Mystery Fiction

Book 2: Willow Falls series

Cover design by Lauren Dingus.

In memory of my cousin
Claudia Kay Henley.

You left the party *way* too soon.

And always, for Steven.

In Dogs We Trust

1

"Louisa! What do you mean you have no place to live?"

My cousin Kay slammed her coffee mug down, her expression fierce. A wave of coffee slopped onto the table. I reached over and dropped a paper napkin onto the spreading puddle. Fortunately I know that all this fury usually signifies nothing, it's just Kay being very Kay.

"I told you. The deal fell through on the house I was buying—"

"So postpone the closing on your parents' house until you find another one."

I shook my head and shredded a piece of cinnamon roll. "Can't. You know I've signed a contract. If I renege, then the Cleavers won't have any place to live, then the people buying their house, and it will be a chain reaction that goes on back and back to some widower in Milwaukee who won't be able to move into

1

a nursing home because selling his house fell through and he'll forget to take his pills and he'll end up in the hospital and it will all be my fault."

Kay's brow furrowed in concentration as she tried to follow my reasoning. She shook her head and picked up her coffee again. "I'm not even going to pretend I understood that."

"I—"

She glared at me and I slumped back in my seat.

"You have to move out of your house by the end of the month, right?" I nodded. She took a sip of coffee. "And the house you were buying is no longer available."

"Right. I've got to start all over looking for a house to buy." I was careful to keep the secret relief I felt out of my voice.

"You've been looking since November. You must have seen everything that's been on the market and probably some that weren't, if I know that Earlene."

I myself suspected that Earlene, my real estate agent, had terrorized a couple of people into showing me a house that they didn't really want to sell. "The bottom line is, I haven't seen anything I want to live in, and I've got to put all my stuff somewhere while I keep looking. And I've got to find a place to stay while I'm doing it."

"Well, obviously you'll stay with me."

I looked at her with a raised eyebrow.

"Oh. Yeah." Kay looked around the café until she spotted Cleta, our favorite waitress, pouring coffee for the mayor at the counter. "Right."

Kay's apartment over her store, OKay Antiques, is small, but perfectly adequate to house her and a visitor. I keep a few changes of clothes in her little back bedroom and have spent a fair number of nights there since I inherited my parents' house and moved back to Willow Falls several months ago. But five days earlier Cleta's house burned down and I gave up my place at Kay's to her.

Two minutes earlier, Cleta had delivered our breakfasts to us at our corner booth at the Bluebird Café. She was wearing a borrowed, too-large cardigan over her shirtwaist dress, the dress she'd been wearing when the call had come that her house was on fire.

"Cleta does not need any more hassles right now," I said in a low voice, adding a dollop of cream to the tea in my cup.

Kay sat up straighter. I knew what was coming. "Hey, you can stay with Bob," she said brightly.

"Kay, leave it," I commanded. I took a big bite of my cinnamon roll.

She gave me a saucy look. "Oh, come on. I bet he's asked you."

I shrugged and swallowed. "None of your business, Miss Nosy. I'm not ready to live with Bob and that's that. Haven't we had this conversation about six times already? I have a better idea. You move in with Ed. Then I can have your place."

"Even if we were currently speaking to each other, you know perfectly well that I wouldn't last one night in his house. His mother would put strychnine in my coffee at dinner and then dance at my funeral."

3

"Yeah, that's true. Then Ed would be faced with the moral dilemma of whether to arrest his mother or not. And except for berating him about you, she makes him far too comfortable for him to arrest her. You're right. You're safer in your own place."

I took another bite of the hot roll. Warm spices blended into the soft yeast of the bread and the sharp sweetness of the cream cheese frosting skimmed over its surface. It was to die for. Or perhaps a good reason to live.

Silence fell over our booth while we ate. The bell over the front door jangled and a moment later a familiar baritone voice called out, "Kay, Louisa, good morning!"

"Hey, Ambrose," we said in unison, then grinned at each other and locked pinkies for a moment. Ambrose slid into our booth next to Kay.

"'Twas a lovely mornin' before, and the sight of the pair of you makes it positively glorious," he declaimed in a fake Irish brogue. Kay bumped him with her shoulder.

"You are such a smoothie," she said. "But it won't work. I'm not giving you a deep discount on that Stickley sideboard in my apartment. I love it and I'm not selling it."

Ambrose is a decorator, a very good one, and he and Kay do a lot of business together. He widened his eyes into an innocent gaze and placed a hand over his heart. "You wound me to the quick. I would never attempt to part you from a piece of furniture that has won your heart."

4

"I saw how you were looking at it when you thought my back was turned," she said gravely, shaking her head.

"Nonsense. I was just admiring your display of bibelots on top of the sideboard. I was inspired by the juxtaposition of the glass orbs and the bowl of feathers."

We were diverted by Cleta, arriving with a fresh carafe of coffee and a mug for Ambrose. He smiled at her gratefully. "Ah, Miss Cleta. Still in the lifesaving business, I see."

"I suspect I was a Newfoundland dog in my last life," she nodded. "I have dreams of pulling drowning sailors to shore with them hanging onto my tail. On the whole this may be an easier job. You want your usual?" Ambrose nodded. "Louisa, how you doin' on water in that pot?"

I lifted the lid off my teapot and looked in. "I could use another hit, it's getting pretty strong."   "You got it," she said and headed for the kitchen. Ambrose watched her go, then turned back to us.

"How is she doing?" he asked in a low voice.

"Pretty good, considering," Kay said. "She still wakes up in the middle of the night, but I think a lot of that is having to deal with the insurance company. Of course she's always worked all the hours on earth, so that hasn't changed."

"At least she has a handy place to stay," he commented.

"Yes, but that brings us to our current topic of discussion," Kay said.

"Which is?"

5

"The fact that Louisa is about to become homeless."

I scowled at her over the bite I was ready to pop into my mouth. It sounded worse when she said it. "The deal fell through on the house I was planning to buy," I explained, "and the closing on my parents' house is still happening. But I'll find somewhere to stay."

"When did this happen?" he demanded. " I leave town for three days to visit a friend and your lives fall to pieces in my absence." Ambrose's friend is a highway patrolman named George Smith who lives about sixty miles away in another small town. They are somewhat more than friends and whenever their schedules allow they go off together for a long weekend.

Cleta reappeared with Ambrose's breakfast—two poached eggs on a nest of steamed fresh spinach, a dollop of cheesy grits, and a separate plate with a pair of golden biscuits steaming on it. "Here you go." She slid the plates in front of him. "Let's see, butter and jam are on the table. Looks like you're all set." She reached around into the vacant booth behind us, purloined a set of flatware wrapped in a large paper napkin and plunked it down beside his plate.

Her other hand grasped a pot of bubbling water. In my experience, Cleta is rare among restaurant people in her understanding that tea must be brewed with boiling water. "Louisa, let me at that pot."

I lifted the lid and pushed the china pot toward her. Steam billowed as she poured a shining stream into the potent brew. "Thanks," I told her, "it was getting strong enough to take over Argentina."

6

"I don't know how you can tell with all that cream you put in it," my cousin the black coffee drinker sniffed.

I ignored her. Pouring cream in my tea let me pretend I was English and cultured for that brief moment I was handling the cream pitcher. Which I knew better than to admit. I wanted to enjoy my fantasies. Of course if I were really English it would be milk in the pitcher, not cream, but the cream was already on the table.

"Now, now," said Cleta, "you leave your cousin alone. A dab of cream in her tea is perfectly harmless and you know it." She winked at me before hurrying back behind the counter, where she set down the water pot and grabbed a coffee mug in one sleek motion. The cup ended on the counter in front of a woman who had just settled onto her usual stool: Eileen, owner of Trellis Island, the garden art store down the street from Kay's.

I poured some of the revived brew into my cup, and then ostentatiously poured in some cream. Kay was watching. I stuck my tongue out at her just a little. She flared her nostrils back at me. Then we both laughed.

"Honestly," Ambrose said. "I don't think either of you has matured one speck since the day I met you, and that was in—good lord, when was it? Could it possibly have been 1964? I think it was." He paused to look surprised. "It's way too early to think of how long ago *that* was."

He broke off a piece of biscuit and added a morsel of blackberry jam before popping it into his mouth.

7

"Mmmm," he breathed, closing his eyes for a moment. "The perfect biscuit, and right here in Willow Falls."

"Anyway," I said, moving the conversation back to its earlier topic, "I'm going out with Earlene this morning to look at a couple more houses, so who knows, maybe I won't be homeless at all."

Kay nodded. "Could happen. And hey, maybe I'll win the lottery while you're out buying a house. Of course I haven't bought any lottery tickets, but that doesn't cut the odds by much. They're still about the same as Earlene finding you a house this morning, or ever from what she's been showing you."

"Hey, she tries," I defended my agent, though my heart wasn't in it. "She can't exactly force my dream house to be on the market just because I decided to move."

Ambrose took a sip from his coffee mug. "You're welcome to stay in my lake cabin as long as you want, but I have to admit it's pretty chilly out there this time of year."

"It's got heat in it, doesn't it?" Kay asked.

"Only the fireplace. My uncle was big on roughing it, and although I improved the interior somewhat I've never bothered to upgrade its basic systems."

Ambrose's idea of improving the interior included a tinkling Waterford chandelier in the bathroom, but the place was truly gorgeous. It enveloped you in comfort, as long as the weather wasn't too cold. I somehow couldn't see myself building fires day and night.

"Thanks," I told him. "I'm afraid the lack of heat could be a problem in February, but it's great to know I have someplace if I need it."

Just then Cleta came back. She looked odd with nothing in her hands; she nearly always held a coffee pot or a plate of something. "Move over for a minute, willya?" she said to me.

I shifted toward the window and she slid in beside me. "So. I just wanted to tellya that I'm going to move out of Kay's place, so you can stay there until you find another house."

I gaped at her. "What?"

"Eileen was talking to Marcello who'd been talking to Earlene who said you won't be buying the MacIlhenny place, but I know the Cleavers are still planning to move into your house at the end of the month because they've hired Benny and his boy to help them move, and Benny didn't say anything about postponing their move when he was here for breakfast. I figured you've had time to tell Kay by now. You wouldn't want her to hear about it from anyone else. You know how she is."

"And how is that?" Kay inquired mildly. "Don't forget she's sitting right here listening to you."

Cleta ignored her. "So you're going to need a place to stay, and that ought to be with Kay, so I'll find somewhere else."

"Hey, Cleta, I need some more coffee!" someone called from the other end of the café.

She leaned out of our booth and hollered back, "Hold your horses, Jeff. I'll be there in a minute. You've had about enough caffeine already anyway."

9

She straightened and looked around the booth at Kay and Ambrose and me. We all started to speak at the same time, our voices blending into a completely incomprehensible noise. Cleta held up a hand. "Stop. You first." She pointed at me.

"No way. You're staying at Kay's until your house gets rebuilt. I can stay at Ambrose's cabin."

"Yeah, and freeze to death," she countered. "Now you." She looked at Kay.

"I want you to stay. It's close to the Bluebird, you're no trouble—"

I tried to ask when I was ever any trouble but she kept going.

"—and if we have to we can make Louisa sleep on the sofa. You're staying."

Cleta pursed her lips and thought for a moment, then pointed to Ambrose. "And what was your two cents?"

"I have an idea I need to check out first. But if it pans out Louisa would be off the streets for at least a couple of weeks."

Cleta nodded and slid out of the booth. "Okay, Ambrose, check on it. Louisa, you've still got nearly two weeks before the closing on your house, right? I'll hang in at Kay's until then and we can fight over it some more when the time comes. And Kay, thanks for everything."

She clumped off in her enormous cross-trainers, calling down the room, "You still need that coffee, Jeff?"

"Yes, ma'am," we heard his meek reply.

Kay and I turned back to Ambrose. "Okay, so what is this idea you've got?" Kay demanded.

He shook his head. "Just a thought. Let me see if anything comes of it. I'll tell you as soon as I know."

I looked at my watch. "Uh oh. I've got to change clothes before Earlene picks me up." I pulled out some money and left it on the table, then slid along the bench and stood up. "Do you need me at the store this afternoon?"

Kay shook her head. "Nah, it should be a quiet day. Stay home and do some packing."

"I can hardly wait," I told them glumly. "Later when I'm not in a hurry I want you to remind me why it was I wanted to move. I can no longer remember." Kay opened her mouth to reply. "Later," I told her, and waved to Cleta as I headed out the door.

2

I went straight home to put on house-hunting clothes. I tried to wear something for these expeditions decent enough to imply that I can actually afford to buy a house, yet comfortable for checking out basement corners or a roof. Not that I ever actually intended to get too close to a basement corner or climb on a roof. But with the right clothes on, I can assure myself that I would certainly be able should the need arise.

I was glad that Kay had not picked up on my relief that I wouldn't be buying the McIlhenny's house. It had seemed attractive enough when I first saw it, and my offer had been quickly accepted. But severe buyer's remorse had set in almost immediately. I just felt wrong about that house, and I couldn't put my finger on why. The truth finally dawned on me when I was sketching the floor plan for Kay while we talked about what furniture I might need to add to what I already owned. As I drew on the back of a flyer for a local dinner theatre production that I'd plucked out of the recycling basket, I suddenly wasn't sure if I was drawing the plan of the house I was buying, or the place where I'd lived in Seattle. That's when I saw that my feelings of discomfort stemmed from the similarity to rooms in which I'd spent many miserable years with my late husband Roger.

I had stopped drawing and stared at the floor plan, feeling like an idiot for not seeing earlier how alike the two houses were. Differences in furniture, wall coverings and carpet, and the pictures on the walls had kept me from seeing the bones of the place. Once I moved in my own belongings the similarity would be inescapable, no matter how I arranged things. The last thing I needed were daily reminders of Roger and the sterile years of our marriage.

But I had signed a contract. Trying to get out of it because I would be reminded of my late husband was not something I was prepared to explain. And I didn't want to lose the several thousand dollars of earnest money tied up in the deal. Then the day before, Earlene had called to tell me the bad news that the sellers were reneging. She asked how I wanted to proceed against them. I was able to say airily, "Oh, just let it go. I'm sure they have good reasons." I could hardly keep my voice even and not start shouting with joy. I did break into a little victory dance when I hung up the phone.

I glanced at the bedside clock as I opened the closet. Earlene would be along in twenty minutes, and she was invariably punctual. Emily Ann, my greyhound, climbed onto the bed and watched as I shucked the outfit I wore and climbed into a pair of wool slacks.

"I had breakfast with your Auntie Kay and told her about us having no house to move into," I told her. "She wanted us to stay with her but she'd forgotten that Cleta is there. Then she said we could move in with Bob and Jack." Jack is Bob's dog.

She thumped her tail at their names.

"I know, but I'm just not ready to live with someone again. It was a disaster when I was married and I'm gun shy. And I like living alone." I pulled on a thin silk turtleneck, then a cotton sweater. "I mean, I know I'm not alone with you here, but that's different."

I drifted into a mental comparison of how wonderfully different it was to live with Emily Ann instead of Roger. With a start I realized I'd stopped moving. I sat down on the bench at the end of the bed to pull on wool socks and sturdy boots. I paused in lacing them up to reach over and stroke Emily Ann's sleek head. "I do like Bob a lot. But I really like having time to myself. And with just you."

She pricked up her ears and turned her long nose toward the bedroom door. Five seconds later the horn from Earlene's car blasted the morning quiet.

"Right on time." I picked up a heavy wool cardigan and pulled it on as I walked down the hall to the front door. Emily Ann followed. "Okay, Emily Ann, I hope I won't be gone too long. You take a nap while I'm out. Just let the machine answer the phone if anyone calls."

My real estate agent, Earlene Hofenstadter, was like someone you'd vote for in a presidential election: you didn't like her a whole lot, but she was the least evil choice on offer. She was very short, barely topping five feet, but her personality was fierce. Her strength as an agent was her undoubted skill in negotiating the best deal for her client. Her weakness was her complete inability to imagine what kind of house a client might want to actually live in.

Perhaps I do her an injustice. Maybe it was just me she didn't understand. And to be fair, how could she divine my desires out of thin air and produce the perfect home in a town the size of Willow Falls? Even I had no idea what kind of house I wanted. All I knew for sure was that I needed something completely my own. A house that did not speak of my dead husband, and hadn't been my parents' home for many years. And I meant what I'd said to Emily Ann about liking time to myself. I was nowhere near making any kind of permanent living arrangement that included Bob. What we had was special, and I wanted to keep it that way.

I started looking for a house in late November. Four months later, my hunting trips with Earlene had fallen into a pattern. She would pick me up in her SUV, sunglasses perched on her nose, her beautiful dark hair pulled back with a large tortoiseshell clasp. She sat with a cushion behind her back, and had extenders on the pedals so she could reach them. We careened about the county, stopping at any house for sale that I hadn't already seen and rejected.

15

The first time I'd seen her in the large car I'd blinked at the incongruity between her size and the vehicle's, but she handled the thing like she'd taken driver's ed on a southern California freeway. By now I was beyond terror when she drove. I just strapped myself in and hunkered down for the ride. If there was to be any kind of car-to-car combat, I had absolutely no doubt that Earlene would come out on top.

This morning, Earlene was all smiles as I climbed into the passenger seat and clicked the seat belt. "Louisa! Good morning! Isn't it just a beautiful day? I thought we'd take a look at two places today, if you have time. One of them isn't too far from your cousin's shop so we'll go there first." By now we were flying down my street and around the corner. "It may be a just a little small, but I always think you can do so much with some good storage pieces and painting the walls a light color." She changed lanes to swoop around a pickup truck and charged through the end of a yellow light. "Of course it wouldn't have to be white. I always think a pale, pale yellow looks good in most houses. Some whites are just too stark, if you know what I mean, and that soft buttery shade of yellow is cheerful but still opens things up. Of course, there's yellow and there's yellow. My sister Gina painted her kitchen all by herself not too long after she got married."

I'd never met Gina in person, but I was sure I'd know her anywhere from her sister's stories.

"They were living in a little garage apartment on Locust Street, and the landlord said it was okay for her to paint," Earlene remembered. "He even gave them credit for part of the month's rent since Gina did all the work. Unfortunately he also let her pick out the paint color. Well, she wanted yellow. It was sort of a dark beige when they moved in, almost a brown really. I can't say I blame her for wanting something a little more cheerful. So she went down to the hardware store and picked out the brightest yellow she could find. Of course we were young then and she didn't know that paint dries darker than you think it will. It's impossible to know how it will end up from those little bitty samples. She worked really hard and did a very nice job. She was just worn out when she finished, so I made her take a shower and took her out to the Dairy Queen to get something to eat. Well, we sat there and ate, and we were still hungry so we ordered more French fries. We were in no hurry to get back to that paint smell. We each got a malt and we ate some more. We were gone a couple of hours. Then I took her home and we walked into that kitchen—" she took a deep breath for dramatic emphasis as she swept around a corner— "and when we turned on the light we needed sunglasses. That was the brightest yellow I have ever seen inside a building. I tell you what, Louisa, you could have driven a school bus into that kitchen and you would have been tripping over it because it would have been so perfectly camouflaged you'd never know it was there."

She braked for a red light, throwing me against my seat belt. She flipped on her left turn signal and when the light changed she accelerated around the corner before the oncoming car could get moving. I didn't see who the other driver was but if it was someone local I figured they knew to stay put until Earlene was out of the way. We hurled downhill for the next block, and just before the bottom of the hill she swung to the curb. She threw open her door and jumped down, ignoring the blast from the horn of the car that she'd almost creamed with her door. I followed more slowly and looked around, finally spotting a small 'for sale' sign in the window of a strange little building on the corner.

The one story structure, built of square stone blocks, clung to the side of the hill. The front wall came up to the sidewalk. A false front stair-stepped up to echo the slant of the sidewalk, ending abruptly where once it must have attached to another building. A vacant lot next door gaped like a missing tooth. The building was narrow, maybe fifteen feet wide, and the front door was centered between two windows that went to each corner.

A faint memory stirred. I had a friend in elementary school, Lila, whose grandmother had lived around the corner from here. For Lila's eighth birthday, her grandmother invited her bring a friend over after school. I don't know if Lila's parents weren't the type to make a fuss over birthdays, or perhaps since her birthday fell on a school day they were waiting for the weekend for any major festivities. In any case, Lila and I had spent a lovely afternoon playing dress up at her grandmother's house. Her grandmother had given each of us a whole quarter to take to the corner store to buy candy. We felt terribly glamorous in our long dresses, though the glamour was tempered by the sight of our school shoes peeping out from the hems. Her grandmother said we would be safer on the steep hill without our too-big dress up shoes.

We did our best to out-gracious each other. I spent my quarter on Lila and she spent hers on me. The lady behind the counter called us both 'moddom' and asked us where she could get a lovely outfit like ours.

"Did this used to be a little neighborhood grocery?" I asked Earlene.

"Yes, it was! Fancy you remembering that. When the supermarkets came in, they just couldn't keep this place going, so they converted it into a residence." Earlene had the door unlocked by now.

My happy childhood memory didn't survive past the front door. Whoever had converted the place had had a love affair with cheap dark paneling. The only light in the first room came from the windows flanking the door. The curtains needed for privacy would make the place as dark as a cave.

However, curiosity always makes me walk through each room. After the living room was a tiny dining room, then a tiny kitchen, then a little passage with a small bathroom on one side and some storage shelves on the other, and finally a tiny bedroom. A door on the far wall opened into a dank paved courtyard that ended at a detached garage.

I turned back to Earlene. She was shaking her head. "No, no, this is awful. I thought maybe you'd want to see it because you like things that are different, but I wouldn't sell this to my worst enemy. You could spend thousands on fixing it up, it needs bigger windows for one thing, and you'd still have an

19

eight hundred square foot dump. I'm sorry, Louisa, I should not have wasted your time on this."

I was touched. She had never said anything bad about any place she'd ever shown me. When I thought about it, her unflagging cheerfulness was amazing. Possibly demented, but still. "You're right, Earlene, it is way too small. But I think I might like something really different and unusual. Whatever happened to people fixing up old barns to live in or silos or caves or something?"

She laughed as she led the way back out. "Honey, they might have been fixing up silos out on the west coast, but here in Willow County we went on keeping silage in them. But you know, somewhere is that house you're going to love, and we are going to find it!"

3

I lounged on the sofa in my living room with Emily Ann, enjoying a book after lunch. The phone rang. I ignored it until I heard Kay's voice boom through the answering machine.

"Hey! Lou! Pick up the phone! How long does it take you to get down the hall to your bedroom?"

I hastened down the hall to pick up. Her harangue continued.

"I don't know why you never put in more extensions. I've wasted hours of my life waiting for you to pick—"

I grabbed the receiver. "Thank you, I don't need any more phones in my life. You have more than enough for both of us."

"That doesn't do much good since only one of us keeps them nearby," she retorted.

Our discussion about the place of the telephone in our lives is ongoing. I can't say we've agreed to disagree since that would imply that we no longer talk about it. "Did you call me up simply to berate me about my attitude toward this instrument of the devil?"

"Nah, that's just the icing on the cake." I could hear her grin and since she couldn't see me I smiled too. "I just called to see if you need any more boxes. If you're going to insist on letting the Cleavers move in at the end of the month, you've got to get busy packing."

"Yes, Kay, I actually do know this." I could hear the testiness in my voice, but either she didn't notice, or didn't care. I love my cousin, but there are times when she finds my last nerve and stomps on it.

"You would let this happen in the shortest month of the year, and not even a leap year. Sheesh. Good planning, cuz."

"Would you like to recite the thirty days hath September rhyme at me, too?"

"Nah, you don't have time for that. Eileen at Trellis Island just got in a shipment of wind chimes. She said she's got a bunch of good boxes for you."

"Tell her to hang onto them. I'll pick them up in the morning."

"I already got them from her. I'll bring them over when I close the store. Oh, wait, there's a city council committee meeting. You can get them tomorrow."

"Okay."

"Gotta go. Talk to you later."

"I'll certainly be looking forward to it." She missed my sarcasm, as she'd already hung up.

My second grade teacher, Miss Irwin, once told me in a moment of frustration that I was contrary. I had no idea what the word meant and had been terrified by how awful it sounded. Now I did know, and I feared that her assessment of my character had been right on target. "Emily Ann!" I called my dog. She trotted down the hall to see what I wanted. "Come on. Let's get your leash and I'll take you for a walk in the park."

4

The next afternoon I let myself in the back door of Kay's store, Emily Ann at my heels. She left my side and went through to greet my cousin while I shed my coat.

"Bring me some coffee, will you?" Kay called. I headed for the coffee maker and filled her favorite mug, then carried it into the store and set it down on the sales counter.

"Thanks." She picked up the mug and took a sip. "It's been so quiet I'm falling asleep."

I looked around. A couple of customers browsed contentedly, murmuring to each other over a variety of items. They looked unlikely to buy anything.

"The coffee looks like it's been stewing all morning," I said, "so that ought to help. You going to work on the books?"

"Yup." She sipped again. "But before I start I want to know if you found a house yesterday. If you did I'm going right out for those lottery tickets."

"Save your money," I told her. "Your prediction about the odds was about right. Earlene took me way out into the country to see a horse farm—"

I heard her snort with laughter. "A horse farm! You?"

"I know. I've always admired horses but I never had much luck around them."

She laughed harder. "Oh, god, remember the time Tonya Bonnet's horse stepped on your foot? Oh, oh, and the time you begged Bradley Oppenheimer for a ride on his pony, even though you were taller than the pony, and when you climbed on its back you overbalanced and fell off the other side into that mud puddle."

The two shoppers looked over at the sound of her laughter.

"Shush," I commanded. "If anyone hears this your days are numbered."

"Well, it wasn't me who told the entire 4-H club about it," she reminded me.

"Whatever happened to Brad? Him and his big mouth."

"Didn't I tell you? He was elected to the state senate—"

"People voted for Bradley *Oppenheimer*?" I was aghast.

"—but then he was convicted of taking bribes from special interests. He managed to get a shorter sentence because he blabbed about everyone else who was in on it."

"I'm not surprised." I shook my head. "Oh, and before the horse farm Earlene took me to see this funny little place that used to be a store."

"Not the little neighborhood grocery over on Sycamore and Seventh."

"That's the one."

"My god, that Earlene woman is demented!"

"Why? She just thought—" Somehow I didn't want anyone to criticize Earlene but me.

"That place is a dump. It was rented to some trashy twenty-year-old boys for the past year, until the old lady who owned it died. Her daughter inherited the place. They say when she went to check on it she needed a gas mask to walk inside."

"Well, it's been cleaned up. It wasn't dirty, just tiny and dark and not a place I'd want to live. I'm not sure Emily Ann and I could both be in the bedroom at the same time."

"So you're still looking. Maybe Ambrose's idea will pan out."

"Maybe. I wonder what it is."

"He could have a line on a little old lady who needs a companion while she's traveling around the world. You might end up in the lap of luxury. He has the most amazing contacts of anyone I know."

"Sounds good to me."

The two shoppers drifted to the door. I called out, "Come see us again."

They turned to give a friendly wave. As one reached for the door it opened, Ambrose filling the

26

doorway. He stepped back, holding the door open, and bowed them out. Then he hurried in. His expression had a distinct cat and canary quality. "Good, you're both here," he said.

"We were just talking about you," Kay told him.

He unwound a heavy silk muffler, his concession to winter weather. He rarely wore anything heavier than a wool sport coat and this muffler. On really Arctic days he added a pair of cashmere gloves, which he owned in about seventeen colors. "Saying lovely things, I trust."

"We were speculating on your bright idea for where Louisa can stay when she has to move out."

Laugh lines crinkled his face. "Good timing. What did you come up with?"

"Kay thinks you must know a little old lady who needs a companion for her world travels." I felt my heart start to beat a little faster.

"No, not that. But I do have something. Guess again."

"You've gotten a commission to redecorate the White House and you'll be in Washington for six months. You need a house sitter. No?"

Ambrose shook his head. "I wish. Guess again."

"You have invested in a cheese making enterprise in Nevada and you need someone to guard the cheese caves," I ventured.

He laughed. "Where do you come up with these things? You might as well just let me tell you."

"Okay, we give up," said Kay agreeably. "Tell us?"

"I have a place for Louisa to stay for at least a couple of weeks. Not only that, it should be fun as well."

Kay sat up straighter on her stool. I looked away for a moment, feeling my heart rev a little more and my lips tighten. My definition of fun might not be entirely the same as Ambrose's. I took a deep breath.

"Where?" I asked, just as Kay said, "Fun doing what?"

"Louisa, you get to be an innkeeper. You're going to run a bed and breakfast while the owner is away."

"A bed and breakfast? Me?" I said, frowning.

And at the same moment Kay exclaimed, "A bed and breakfast? *Louisa*?"

I turned to glare at her. She didn't have to sound quite so incredulous.

Ambrose nodded. "I think I've mentioned my friend Mary Pat who runs the Bunny Farm Inn out near my lake cabin?"

Kay nodded. I shook my head. I'd never heard of this Mary Pat

"Mary Pat was on the waiting list for a tour of English B&Bs. Some innkeepers' association organizes it and they only take a few people at a time."

"There are groups of antiquers that do that too," Kay put in. "Can't you see a bunch of us all fighting for the same deals?"

"Innkeepers might just be a tad less competitive," Ambrose said. "But getting back to the point—" he primmed his mouth at Kay, "Mary Pat just found out there's a space for her. Someone dropped out or something. So she needs someone to baby-sit her inn." He beamed at me.

I looked from Ambrose to Kay and back to Ambrose. "Innkeeper? Me?"

Kay had a light in her eyes I knew well. "That is perfect," she enthused. "Louisa can play innkeeper and still keep house hunting."

Visions rampaged through my brain of broken water pipes, a large old-fashioned house burning down, an unruly group of travelers shouting at me because there was no room for them at the inn. I went on to a scenario in which my phone was ringing at midnight because pillows weren't properly plumped, and then another call because the husband staying in the Tartan Suite just had a heart attack in delicato— in the Rosebud Room.

Without being unduly pessimistic, I've always felt the old saw that whatever can go wrong will go wrong is based on a great deal of truth.

"This time of year it will really be more like house sitting," Ambrose assured me.

"Yeah?" I gave him a skeptical look.

"Not many people think of taking late-winter vacations in the Midwest. I doubt if you'll have more than a handful of guests during the whole time you're there. Maybe not any. It will be a piece of cake."

"Doesn't sound like a very lucrative enterprise," Kay said. "How does she stay open? Why not just close the place while she's gone?"

"I think she does have a few people booked," Ambrose admitted.

"Even a handful will expect breakfast at a bed and breakfast," I said, emphasizing the B words with a certain amount of sarcasm. "I don't want to spend my declining years scrambling eggs for a bunch of strangers."

Kay snorted, "Declining years? You're only a year older than me and I'm not declining."

"Ten months, not a year," I corrected. "And there's the bed part too, they'll expect me to make their beds and clean up after them."

Ambrose's good humor remained unimpaired. "Oh, come on, Louisa, what's a bed or two to straighten? Mary Pat offers a sort of glorified continental breakfast, which is right up your alley. I know you can bake because I've tasted your breads and cookies. And someone comes in to help with the housework."

"It's not just that," I said, and stopped. I needed time to think, so I could figure out why this felt like such a bad idea.

"She'll have to go off and brood about this," Kay interjected. "But don't worry, she'll do it." I leaned over to give her shoulder a push which nearly unseated her from her tall stool. She pushed back. We scuffled for a minute like a couple of kids.

"Children, children, am I going to have to separate you?" Ambrose shook his head.

"She started it," said Kay. I made a face at her.

"Just come and talk to Mary Pat," Ambrose begged. "She can give you the best idea of what you'd be getting yourself into, and then you can decide."

"Well, okay," I said, and won one of his amazing smiles, complete with full blue-eyed twinkle.

He uses that smile to train the customers of his interior design business, nudging them with it in the direction he knows they ought to go and away from disastrous color choices and furniture they'll soon tire of. "Atta girl."

"When are we talking about doing this?" I asked. Maybe I could stall until I thought of an excuse.

"Let me call Mary Pat and see if we can get together late this afternoon," he offered. "I'll drive you out there. It will easier than explaining how to find the place. Will you be home later, or here at the store?"

"Home," Kay said firmly before I could open my mouth. "She still has a hell of a lot of packing to do if she has to move out in a week."

I gave her a frosty look before raising my chin and telling Ambrose, "I will be at home. I have a great deal of packing to do in the next week."

After Ambrose left I roused Emily Ann from her nap on a velveteen-covered settee. "Come on, Miss Pup, we're going home."

She climbed down, stretched her long legs and followed me to the back door. Kay was loading flattened boxes into the back of my car.

"This ought to hold you for today," she told me. "Do you have enough tape to put them back together?"

"I got more yesterday," I assured her. "Is there room for Emily Ann in there?"

"She can lie on top of the boxes."

Emily Ann had other ideas. She looked into the back of the car, then at me. Her lowered ears radiated

31

disapproval. "It's a stack of boxes," I told her. "Your Auntie Kay says you'll be all right on top of them."

She gazed at Kay, then stalked to the passenger door. I opened it for her and pushed the seat back as far as it would go. She got in and sat with her rump on the seat and her front feet on the floor. Let's go, she seemed to be saying, I can't sit like this forever.

"Right." I closed the door and turned to give Kay a brief wave before climbing into the car. We pulled out of the parking spot. Kay hugged herself against the cold as we drove away.

"Were you listening to what Ambrose told us?" I asked Emily Ann. I turned out of the alley onto Second Street. "You won't believe the hare-brained idea he's come up with." Emily Ann perked up her ears. She's always interested in hares. "He thinks I should take care of his friend's bed and breakfast while she's away."

I peeked over at her. Her head was cocked at a quizzical angle. "Okay, you probably think bed and breakfast sounds good. In people terms, a bed and breakfast is usually a quaint old house with more rooms than the owner knows what to do with. So they fix it up, usually with eighteen different flowered fabrics in every room and lots of antique furniture or supposedly antique furniture and a ton of bad old pictures on the walls, and they let people come and spend the night, and in the morning they have to feed everybody. And they have to be very polite all the time to the people who come and stay so they will tell other people how lovely it all was so those other people will want to come and stay and the person who owns the

B&B will make enough money to keep living in their big old house."

Emily Ann blinked her short lashes at me.

"Whose side are you on?" I asked her. "Can you really see me making nice to a bunch of strangers over breakfast and answering questions about what there is to do in Willow County in February? *That* would be the world's shortest conversation."

Emily Ann gave a ladylike little snort; I wasn't sure if it was a sneeze or a comment.

"And it's not just the breakfasts. I'm sure they won't make their own beds or clean their bathrooms. I don't even like cleaning up after myself. And what if they just hang around the house all day, like unwanted relatives?"

She looked very wise. I couldn't help chuckling. "I guess you could demonstrate how to take naps, huh. You're the right dog for that job." As I said it, I suddenly saw that my problem was solved. I couldn't stay anywhere Emily Ann couldn't be with me, and who would want an innkeeper, however temporary, who arrives with a seventy-five pound dog in tow?

"That's it!" I exclaimed. "Emily Ann, you've saved the day. I still don't know where we're going to stay until we find another house, but I bet you a dog biscuit that this Mary Pat is going to regretfully decline the services of Miss Emily Ann Dog at her foofy B&B."

5

"What a pity it gets dark so early this time of year," Ambrose said. "You won't be able to fully appreciate Mary Pat's location until you see it in the daylight."

"I've never noticed this inn," I told him. "Of course I don't spend a whole lot of time at Parsons Lake."

I saw his smile flash in the light from the dashboard. "Ah, Louisa's famous distaste for the woods."

"Only when they attack me," I defended myself, "which of course seems to be about two seconds after I step foot off the path, if there is one. But I've never been much for lakes either. I like to swim, but not with fish. Ig. They're intimidating."

"Now there I agree with you. I'm afraid if I'd come upon the fish that gave the three wishes, both the fish and I would have just been out of luck."

"Oooh, I know. Can you imagine picking one up with your bare hands and throwing it back in the water? There must be a reason they breathe water and we breathe air. We were never supposed to lay eyes on each other. But you were telling me about Mary Pat's inn. Where the heck is it?"

"The location is part of its charm. It's on an island about two hundred feet off shore. You park on this side, walk over the bridge, then Mary Pat picks you up in the island's car, or you take a golf cart. Guests get keys to the carts when they arrive."

"You must be joking." Mentally I was thanking Emily Ann again for saving me from any possibility of staying at this place.

"No, no, it's really quite fun."

"But what about when it snows? I don't imagine golf carts are of much use then." I saw myself frozen solid, under a mound of snow dumped onto my golf cart when a tree limb got fed up and shed its load.

"Well, true, but then how much snow do we get? Maybe four good ones a year. And this has been such a warm winter that the lake isn't really even frozen."

"The lake freezes?" Now I had visions of packs of wolves racing over the ice.

"Usually, but not this year, or at least not entirely. I assume Mary Pat puts snow tires on the is-land's car in the winter, and it's not so far that a person couldn't walk from the house to the bridge."

"I'm sure a lot of people enjoy that sort of thing," I said. I didn't think I was destined to be one of them. "How do you know Mary Pat?"

This was mere conversation making. Ambrose knows everyone.

"Oh, we go back *years*. She was a little kid when I first knew her. I don't know if you remember, but my mother and I moved to Willow Falls when I was about thirteen."

I did remember. He had arrived in April to finish out the school year in the eighth grade. I was in seventh grade so we had no classes together, but I had noticed him for the first time in the hall between classes on a rainy Thursday. Tall, blond, dazzling blue eyes. He was being followed by James Hunter, one of the school's bullies, and his two minions, who were swishing their hips as they walked and crooning in a nasty way, "Ambrose! Oh, Ambrose!"

Ambrose had appeared not to hear them. Just before he passed me, he suddenly pivoted and plowed right into James, bringing the heel of his shoe down on the bully's instep and poking stiffened fingers into his gut. As he did he said something low in James' ear. James had turned red and then white and reeled away, his confused buddies following. It happened so fast that it was over before I had blinked twice. Ambrose had turned back around and continued on his way.

"I remember. You beat up James Hunter the first time I saw you."

"Oh, hardly beat him up, Louisa. He just needed to be taught a little lesson. I figured I might as well get it over with."

"It was the highlight of my seventh grade year."

36

"He was a nasty little twerp," Ambrose nodded. "Anyway, I spent that summer out here at the cabin with my uncle, and he took me to the Fourth of July celebration down at Miller's Crossroads. There was a little girl there, maybe five or six years old, who had managed to get hold of about sixteen helium balloons, and she absolutely would not let go of them. Her mother was begging her to share them with the other children, but she had them and she was not sharing with anyone. And that was my first sight of Mary Pat." He chuckled.

"Um, she sounds charming," I lied. This was getting worse and worse.

"Oh, but that was when she was five. By the time she was in high school she did volunteer work in the school library and was a stalwart in the drama club. In fact she starred in every school play for four years. She really is quite an amazing actress. You'll like her, she's charming. Just don't get between her and any balloon she might want." He grinned at me and turned on the left signal. "Here's the turn-off now."

The headlights of his car lit up a sign.

Bunny Farm Inn
Unique Bed & Breakfast Accommodations
1 mile

A wrought-iron arrow pointed to a narrow side road. Ambrose made the turn. We drove down a dark tunnel of road, evergreen trees pressing close on both sides. The road was smooth and well maintained though, and it was only a few minutes before we came

37

to a clearing by the lake. The motion of the car activated a pair of lights; at the edge of the clearing I saw a neatly anonymous garage big enough for two vehicles, with space for about eight cars beside it. Ambrose parked by the garage and we got out.

We trod over crunching gravel. When I saw the footbridge my heart began to accelerate. I don't like bridges. I'm okay in a car—unless the bridge is really high or long—but I avoid walking on them if I can help it.

Stepping onto any bridge zaps me back in time. I am suddenly eleven years old again, which was the age at which I was forced to go to summer camp. Not a happy experience. I was just enough younger than the other campers in my cabin to have nothing in common with them. And I was the only one of the group who loathed normal camping activities. I wanted to like roasting marshmallows on an open fire, but the flaming confection invariably fell off the stick into the dirt or burned my mouth. The ghost stories told in the dark gave me terrible dreams. Gluing twigs onto orange juice cans in the craft class was not my idea of creating a useful or beautiful item. And swimming in the lake was a tense attempt to keep moving so that fish wouldn't bite my toes.

The daily hikes through the woods were the worst, involving not only trees and dirt and bugs but a swinging rope bridge over a roaring creek. My campmates thought it was the height of fun to rock the bridge wildly when I was on it. I was terrified to the point of nausea. Perhaps if I had gone ahead and thrown up on them they might have stopped.

Unfortunately they never got near enough for that expedient to be practicable. So I tried to act like I didn't care and spent as much time as I could alone, hiding in the branches of a big leafy tree that I managed to figure out how to climb. I was in trouble much of the summer for "failing to participate," and the other girls in my cabin alternated between taunting every move and ignoring my very existence.

I survived the experience and perhaps was a stronger person because of it—at least strong enough to threaten self-annihilation so convincingly that I was never sent to camp again. But I was left with a residual fear of bridges, especially if they move while I am crossing.

Which of course this one did. It was some sort of floating contraption, like a very long dock. Ambrose said something about the bridge accommodating different water levels that occur through the year. I hardly heard him for the pounding of my heart in my ears.

The bridge was fairly wide, about six feet, and had handrails on both sides. I took a deep, slow breath, tensed my jaw, and stepped onto the damned thing.

It swayed. My stomach swayed with it.

Keeping my eyes on the connection to land on the other side, I resolutely trod down the middle. I was aware of Ambrose's voice behind me, sounding quite far away. Not a single word of his discourse penetrated my concentration. I didn't know I was holding my breath until I stepped onto solid land and was able to take in air again. The sudden rush of air made little stars swim into my peripheral vision.

"...and so that's how Mary Pat ended up with the family home and turned it into an inn," Ambrose concluded as he drew a key ring out of his pocket.

"How nice," I managed. I hoped the story had not included any shocking revelations that I would be expected to remember.

Enough light spilled across the way from the floods in the parking area for him to select a key. He walked to a nearby shed. The key fitted neatly into a padlock hanging from a hasp on the door. He slid the door open, revealing two golf carts. He backed one out and I clambered in. In a moment we were gliding down a curving paved path.. The cart's little headlights revealed the trunks of bare trees and the occasional evergreen. The motor emitted a smug whirring sound, as though we were riding in a contented Persian cat. In a few minutes we rounded a bend and came in sight of the house.

I gaped at the looming shape. A deep porch wrapped all the way around the lower floor. Wide bay windows flanked the massive double front door, and on the north side of the house a porte-cochère provided a covered side entry. Ambrose pulled the golf cart to a stop by wide front steps, lit by an antique porch fixture that I knew would have Kay salivating.

"Wow," I said, "this is some house."

As we ascended the shallow steps, the left-hand door flew open. Golden light from the foyer streamed out, shadowing the figure of the woman standing there.

Mary Pat Haskell's silhouette was about equally wide as tall. We shook hands in the doorway and murmured greetings, and she turned to lead us into a large living room.

Following her, I thought that she was the most graceful human being I had ever seen. She gestured with one small white hand toward two high backed wing chairs near a crackling fire. Ambrose and I sat, and Mary Pat sank onto a curvaceous Victorian settee near a low, round oak table. On its polished surface rested a tray set with the makings of tea.

I guessed from Mary Pat's unlined face, as well as Ambrose's story about her and the balloons, that she was in her mid forties. She had fluffy brown hair with red highlights, cut to chin length so that it fanned out around her face. Her eyes were the color of chocolate. She was wearing an ankle-length dress of deep green wool, black Mary Janes, and a coral mohair shawl. I couldn't tell if the thick eyelashes and pink cheeks were natural or the result of very skillful make up.

"Mrs. McGuire, how wonderful to meet you," she twinkled at me. She lifted the lid from a large, ornately-decorated china teapot and spooned in a positively alarming amount of tea. "I followed your adventures on the news last fall with great interest. Have you fully recovered from that terrible ordeal?" She hefted a gleaming kettle from an electric hot plate and poured steaming water into the pot.

"Oh, yes," I assured her, as I had so many others, "our fifteen minutes of fame is safely in the past."

"At least until the trial," Ambrose added.

"When will that be?" Mary Pat asked.

"Not for a few more months," I said. "Ambrose and I will have to testify, but there's little doubt of a conviction."

"Thank heavens for that. To think of you fleeing from a murderer in our woods—well, it must have been horrible. Just absolutely horrible."

"It's all over now," I said. I would be glad when everyone forgot what had happened.

"It was fabulous for business though." She beamed at me.

I tried not to look as taken aback as I felt. "Yes?"

"Indeed. I was booked for weeks after the news got out. Our mystery weekend that we hold every Halloween had people literally fighting to get tickets."

"Ah, yes, the proverbial ill wind," Ambrose remarked.

Mary Pat began to search for something on her low table. She made a vexed chirp. "I have forgotten the napkins," she said, shaking her head. "Excuse me for just a moment, won't you?"

She rose and went through wide doors between the room we were in and the dining room behind it, and then through a swinging door that I assumed led to the kitchen. A moment later a loud metallic crash reverberated through the house, then a deep, gruff voice said, "God dammit! Who put that there!" The intervening doors muffled the sounds but they were still quite clear.

Ambrose and I looked at each other. "Who's back there?" I mouthed, for the voice had been much deeper than Mary Pat's.

He made an I-don't-know face. "Maybe a neighbor dropped in or something?" he stage-whispered back.

"A neighbor! Are there other houses out here??"

"Well, no."

"Then we're miles from another house!" I hissed.

Ambrose gave a little nod toward the kitchen to indicate Mary Pat's return. I put on a pleasant expression, ready to commiserate over whatever had fallen in the kitchen.

"Here we are," Mary Pat caroled as she entered the room, waving white linen napkins. "Now we can be messy with complete impunity." She handed each of us a napkin, then resettled on the sofa in front of the tea table. I looked at the square of creamy fabric in my hand. It was large, probably of Victorian vintage, with a hand embroidered monogram. I devoutly hoped not to be the least messy with it.

"Now, where were we?" Mary Pat picked up the tea pot. "Oh, yes, your ordeal with the murderer. You must have been witless with fear. Mrs. McGuire, how do you take your tea?" She gave me an inquiring look.

"Um, one lump and a bit of milk," I said, trying to decide how I felt about being characterized as witless. Apparently there was to be no explanation of the noises from the kitchen. "But please, call me Louisa."

She busied herself with a cup, dropping in a cube of sugar and pouring steaming milk from a small blue earthenware jug. "Thank you, Louisa it shall be. I hope that Indian tea is acceptable to you."

"Yes, I love Indian, thank you." It hadn't occurred to me that it might be Chinese tea, which I can't imagine drinking with milk in it.

43

"Wonderful. This is my own blend of Assam and Darjeeling, with emphasis on the Darjeeling since it never gets bitter." She deftly poured tea through a strainer into the cup. Ambrose rose, took the cup, and set it on the table beside me.

I picked up my cup, mentally biting my tongue. Mary Pat had her teas backwards. In my experience it is Assam that can be brewed without bitterness, but it didn't seem tactful to say so.

"And you, Ambrose?" she asked him, teapot poised to pour again.

"Plain for me," he told her, and smiled at her as she filled his cup. He took it and returned to his chair.

I inhaled the fragrant steam, then took a sip of tea. "Mmmm, this is not only acceptable but wonderful," I said. "I feel positively surrounded by coffee drinkers most of the time. It's always nice to find someone who appreciates tea."

Pleasure blossomed on her face. "I feel exactly the same way. I listen to them ordering coffee in those ubiquitous shops, all that caf decaf short tall foam no foam soy milk nonfat rigamarole—"

"I'd like to know what happened to small, medium and large," Ambrose put in.

"You'd think they were custom building the holy grail and not just getting some bitter-flavored hot water. It just makes me want to fly home and warm the teapot." Mary Pat's cheeks were flushed and her tea cup rattled on its saucer.

"Yes!" I cheered. "Oh, do you know what I saw in the grocery store the other day?"

They looked at me expectantly.

"Aerosol cans of coffee foam."

"No!"

"I swear."

"Oh, for heaven's sake," Mary Pat said, shaking her head. "Fake foam, when you could be having real tea."

"Hear, hear!" added Ambrose, raising his cup in salute. "Ladies, a toast. May the cup at your lips ever hold the finest brew!" He and I clinked the rims of our cups together, then gestured with them toward Mary Pat before sipping. I felt as though I had joined a secret club.

"Of course I do make excellent coffee," Mary Pat went on, "since many of my guests drink the stuff and they get so cranky without it. But I confess I dream of the day we'll be well enough known to cater only to tea drinkers."

"I think it would make for great marketing," Ambrose told her.

"Alas, we're not there yet." Mary Pat settled back and took a decorous sip of her tea.

"Mary Pat, I don't know what Ambrose told you of my circumstances—" I wanted to get the discussion of the impossibility of my taking care of her inn out of the way.

"I understand you're about to become temporarily homeless," she said, shaking her head. "I was surprised to hear of anyone looking for a house to buy in February."

"I know, my timing does seem to be off."

"This is not the most salubrious time of year to be moving, my dear."

"I've been looking for months. I didn't think it would be so difficult to find what I want, or that my parents' house would sell so fast. But homeless or not, I don't think I'm the right person to take care of your inn while you're gone."

The corners of her mouth tightened. "But Louisa, from what I've seen of you so far, you would be quite adequate. You're polite, you seem reasonably intelligent, and I know you're resourceful from the way you dealt with that madman in the fall."

"Well, thank you," I managed. "Adequate" and "reasonably intelligent" rankled a bit. "But you see, I can't possibly come without my dog, and I'm sure you won't want a huge greyhound here."

Mary Pat began to smirk, and then to laugh. Tea sloshed over the rim of the cup she was holding. She set it down and laughed some more. My lips curved automatically in response but my bewilderment must have shown on my face. In a moment she regained control.

"Oh, my dear, I apologize," she said, shaking her head. "How rude of me. It's just that—" a new chuckle forced its way out. "Sorry. Ambrose, you naughty boy, you neglected to tell Louisa about the Bunny Farm."

"I have been remiss. My apologies to you both," he said gravely.

I looked back and forth between them. "What about the Bunny Farm?" A raucous film of what might go on here began to rampage through my brain. Perhaps influenced by Mary Pat's mention of Halloween, it starred a coven of thirteen flying on their broom-sticks over the lake on a moonlit night.

The inn was certainly isolated enough for anything. My thoughts must have shown on my face.

"Oh, we don't do anything like *that* out here," Mary Pat said, making me wonder if she was a mind reader. "No, it's just that bringing your dog would hardly be an issue when one of our claims to fame is that we invite people to bring their dogs along when they visit."

"Really?" It came out a squeak.

"Oh yes. Your dog is the reason Ambrose thought of you when he heard I needed someone to keep the inn for me while I am in England."

"Well, damn," I heard myself say. Mary Pat raised an eyebrow, and I blushed. "Um, I mean—" Mary Pat and Ambrose stared at me. "It's just that I bet Emily Ann a dog biscuit that you wouldn't want me to come because of her, and now I'm not sure if I owe her the biscuit or if I'm going to have to eat it myself."

6

It was Thursday evening before I had a chance to tell Kay about my trip to the Bunny Farm Inn. She heard about an estate she had a chance of buying and rushed off early Wednesday to a small town in Iowa. I minded the store and continued to pack up my house, whenever I could bear to look into the open maw of another box.

Kay returned late Thursday afternoon after I had closed the store, and we arranged over the phone to meet for dinner at the Bluebird. Dinners were a new venture at the café. They had served breakfast and lunch since the café opened, but finally succumbed to our frequent requests to feed us in the evening as well. So far dinners were served Thursday to Saturday, but in the spring Dorothy planned to add more evenings as the tourist traffic increased.

I arrived first and waved to Cleta when I walked in. She waved back from behind the counter and looked around the half-full room. "Take the corner booth," she called to me, pointing. I nodded and she turned back to continue making fresh coffee. I turned to my left and started toward my table.

"Hey, Louisa," said a jovial voice at my elbow. "Where's that fast dog of yours? You look kind of strange without her!"

A middle aged couple occupied the third booth— Dan from the dog park and his wife Mildred. "Hey there, Dan," I said, smiling at him. "I hardly recognize you without mud on your boots and Roxie at your side. Have you already eaten?"

Dan patted his pot belly. "We're waiting for Cleta to bring us dessert."

Mildred pursed her lips. "I certainly don't know where you're going to put it, Dan."

"You know I can always find room for one of the Bluebird's desserts," he assured her. "Besides, I can walk it off tomorrow at the dog park with Roxie."

Dan and I gazed blandly at Mildred, who rarely came out with Dan and their dog. People assume that at the dog park both dogs and people get exercise. We don't, other than walking around with plastic bags looking for evidence of our dogs' digestive systems and throwing balls for the retrievers. The dogs get plenty of exercise. The people stand around and talk about them as they play.

"I hear you're back in the market for a house, Louisa," Mildred said, looking concerned.

I nodded and made a face. "I don't know why I thought I could find one in no time. Guess I've learned my lesson. Well, I'll let you all have your dessert. Kay will be here in a few minutes. Good to see you, Mildred. Dan, give Roxie a pat for me. Kay's making me keep my nose to the grindstone on my packing so I'm not sure if I'll see you at the park tomorrow."

"Better bring Emily Ann along, Louisa, she needs to run," he said, and I nodded in agreement, patted him on the shoulder, and continued on to the last booth. I slid onto the bench facing the door so I could keep an eye out for Kay.

I was studying the menu when the bell over the door signaled Kay's arrival. Her cheeks shone pink from the cold. I waved to her, and she hurried over, calling out greetings as she came. She threw her purse on the seat opposite mine and unwound a long muffler from her neck, bundling that and her coat onto the bench. Then she slid onto the bench. "Brrrr, it's freezing out there," she shivered. "What's for dinner?"

I handed her the menu. "No cinnamon rolls but everything else sounds pretty good. How was your trip?"

She bounced on her seat in excitement. "It was great. There's some decent furniture and the kitchen stuff is wonderful. Wait till you see the quilts. And a gorgeous vintage sewing basket. I took a bunch of pictures, I'll email them to you later tonight."

"Sounds worthwhile. Gosh, I'm hungry."

"Me too." She bent her head to study the menu.

The bell over the door jangled and I looked up idly to see if anyone I knew had come in.

It was Bob. I felt my face split into a huge smile as I sat up straighter. He spotted us and waved and started down the row of booths, pausing a couple of times to greet people he knew.

Kay looked up from the menu and saw my face. "What?" she asked, and looked over her shoulder. "Ah."

It seemed to take forever for him to reach our booth and slide in beside me. He put an arm over my shoulder, said a polite, "Excuse me, Kay," and gave me a rather nice kiss. "Hi there. I missed you," he said.

"Hi yourself," I returned. I didn't seem to have breath left for more than that.

He turned back to Kay. "Hi, Kay, how was your trip?"

"Good," she nodded. "It was good."

"But what are you doing here?" I demanded "I thought you weren't coming over until tomorrow."

He nodded. "I know, but something happened, and I just couldn't wait to tell you."

"See," Kay put in, "if you remembered to carry your cell phone he could have called you right away."

"And wouldn't be sitting next to me now," I retorted, and turned back to Bob. "What's up?"

"You know that hypnosis symposium in California I told you about?" He sounded pleased and excited. I'd been making a study of his voice since I met him in October. His voice and everything else about him.

"The one with all the important people speaking?"

"That's the one. Well, one of those important people just broke a leg in several places and is in traction and they've asked me to fill in."

"Wow, that's great!" I told him. "I mean, that they asked you, not that whoever it was broke their leg. Of course they should have asked you in the first place, but better late than never."

51

"They made the arrangements with the other speakers a year or more ago," he said, "long before our little adventure."

Bob has always done some speaking engagements on his specialty, hypnotic anesthesia, but thanks to CNN and all the other networks he was a lot better known now.

"So when is it? When do you have to go?" I asked him.

"Ah, that's the kicker. I have to leave tomorrow."

"Tomorrow! Tomorrow as in the day after today?"

"Yeah, that tomorrow."

Kay put in, "Wow, talk about being a last minute replacement."

"True. But they're going to treat me very nicely since I'm doing them this great big favor."

"How nicely?" Kay wanted to know.

"Well, plane tickets for two, for one thing."

Oh, damn, I thought. I didn't say anything, and the expression on his face turned to worry. "Louisa, don't you want to come?"

"Yes," I sighed, "I do want to. Of course I do. But I've just gotten roped into helping out a friend of Ambrose's for the next two weeks. She needs a house sitter for her bed and breakfast. Damn. I'd much rather go with you."

"Damn," he repeated, with exactly the right note of disappointment in his voice. "I really want you to come. Can't you tell her you've changed your mind?"

I wrestled with my conscience. "No," I said at last. "I really don't see how I can back out of it."

"Could she put off her trip for a couple of weeks?" Bob asked. "Then you could do both."

I shook my head. "She's going on a tour of English B and Bs. She was on the waiting list and finally got a spot in the group. She'd lose her deposit, besides the disappointment."

"I could find someone else for her," Kay offered. Like Ambrose, she knows everyone.

"Well..." The desire to be on that plane with Bob swelled in my breast. I fought my conscience for a moment, then said, "No, I'm sorry. I just can't. I promised."

"Well, now it won't be nearly as good a trip." Bob sighed. "I was really hoping you'd go with me. I figured Kay could look after Jack and Emily Ann."

"At least I can do that," I said.

"You can have the dogs at this place?" His voice was incredulous.

I started to laugh. "Oh, yes. It's practically a requirement at this one."

He frowned. "Doesn't sound like any B and B I've ever heard of." His voice had an endearingly huffy tone.

Kay looked interested. "Have you stayed in many?"

"Well, there was the one Louisa and I went to before Christmas."

I felt a blush heating my face and looked down, glad the café was dimly lit for dinner. In December we had left Kay in charge of both dogs and flown to Charleston, South Carolina for a long weekend. We intended to walk around, eat southern food, buy gifts for friends and admire the antebellum architecture.

Instead we had used the unusually cold weather as an excuse to stay nearly the whole time in our relentlessly antebellum room.

We'd had a very good time.

"And?" Kay prompted Bob.

"And okay, that's the sum total of my knowledge of the bed and breakfast industry."

"Okay then."

"But the point is, Louisa can't come with me. Damn," he said again.

"I know. I'm really disappointed," I told him. "But you'll do a better job without me there to distract you."

"What makes you think you distract me?" He gave me a sidelong look and waggled an eyebrow just a little.

"I'm just hoping. I know how you distract me." We gazed foolishly at each other until Kay cleared her throat.

"So, Bob," she said, "what time is your flight?"

"I need to be at the airport about 9:30."

"That's do-able," I nodded. The airport is on the far side of High Cross from Willow Falls, but I'm a notoriously early riser.

Cleta appeared at our table then. "Hey, Bob, good to see you. Didn't know you were coming down tonight."

"Couldn't miss dinner at the Bluebird."

"Y'all got enough menus there? Want something to drink?"

"Coffee," said Kay and Bob together. Most Midwesterners drink coffee from morning till bedtime.

54

"Just some water right now," I told Cleta. She nodded and went off for our drinks and we concentrated on the menus. When she came back we gave her our orders and she sped away to the kitchen.

"So you're really going to take care of this inn?" Kay asked me.

I shrugged. "I said I would. Since it's still winter Mary Pat has only a few people booked. Didn't seem to be any reason I couldn't handle it. Someone comes in to help with the housework, and breakfast is a matter of fresh breads and yogurt and cereals. I may not be able to help at the store while I'm there though."

She waved her hand airily at me. "Hey, not to worry. It's still winter for me as well. Not many more tourists in town than out at the lake. I hate it that you can't go with Bob, though. Are you sure you can't tell her you've changed your mind?"

They both looked at me. I had to shake my head. "I really can't. As soon as I said I'd mind the inn she got up and sent the email confirmation that she was going on the trip and charged it to her credit card. I have no idea what her finances are, but I imagine an inn out in the woods like that operates on a pretty narrow margin."

Kay looked at Bob. "And once Louisa gives you her word, that's it. A promise is a promise. Which of course is why she needed somewhere to stay in the first place."

He slid an arm around my shoulders in a hug. "That's one of the things I like about her, she's trustworthy."

We were still exchanging goofy looks when Cleta set a plate in the middle of the table. "Dorothy wants you to try these appetizers and see what you think," she said, deploying small china plates in front of us, each a different pattern. I recognized the plate in front of Bob as one I'd picked up for a quarter at a garage sale and given to Cleta; it showed Mr. Jeremy Fisher the frog in an elegant pose.

"Guinea pigs are us," remarked Kay, and we each slid an appetizer onto our plates. Mine was a square pastry of dough wrapped around a filling that included red cabbage, walnuts, gorgonzola, and some spices. Bob tried a miniature cream puff filled with an herbed cheese. Kay chose a tiny tostada with black beans, fresh salsa, and a bit of sour cream.

"God, these are good," Kay moaned after her first taste. "Who needs the rest of dinner? I could just eat these until they threw me out."

Bob and I both nodded wordlessly and popped more morsels into our mouths. I tasted a warm slice of potato with a dollop of tomato chutney and some crème fraiche.

"So what's the timeline on this inn thing?" Kay asked me in a slightly muffled voice. She too had just dispatched another bite-size wonder.

"I go over tomorrow to learn the ropes--"

"Tomorrow?" asked Bob in an exaggeratedly shocked tone. "Tomorrow as in the day after today?"

I poked him in the ribs. "Tomorrow as in after I take you to the airport, tomorrow. Mary Pat leaves on Tuesday, so I'll go out to stay that morning. I have two ladies and their dog coming on Thursday for a long

56

weekend, and another couple arriving Friday. That's all I know of right now."

"Good thing I booked the moving guys for Monday to get your stuff into storage," Kay said.

I didn't say anything. What had been theoretical was now too close and too real.

Cleta appeared at our table again. "So how were they?"

I looked at the appetizer plate. All the savory little tidbits had disappeared.

"To die for," I assured her. "Maybe you could specialize and serve nothing but appetizers. No one would ever notice that's all there was."

"Oh, they'd notice," she said, picking up the small plates and hurrying off.

"Why is it called the Bunny Farm Inn?" Bob asked me.

Kay nodded. "I wondered about that too."

"So did I. I asked Mary Pat while she was showing me around. She said it used to be a real rabbit farm. Her grandmother raised angora rabbits for their fur. One of her childhood memories is of sitting in a big rocking chair with a rabbit in her lap, petting it to remove the fur that her grandmother spun into yarn."

"That sounds like a nice, soothing occupation, petting rabbits," Kay said. "Louisa, when we get tired of the store, maybe we could do that instead."

"Sounds good to me," I agreed.

Cleta's return was heralded by wonderful smells. She hustled plates onto the table in front of us, then was gone again before I could say thank you. My plate was a vision. Dorothy, the Bluebird's cook, had done something with puff pastry and asparagus, and to the side was a cool concoction that included shredded beets, walnuts, arugula, and slivers of sweet onion. I tasted that and let the orange vinaigrette dressing linger on my tongue. After a moment I breathed out a soft, "Wow," and looked up to see Bob and Kay had dazed expressions on their faces. We all began to eat. From time to time one of us would moan.

When most of his dinner was gone, Bob gave a sigh and sat back. "I'm inhaling this food," he said. "Good grief, why am I leaving town?"

"They're only open here three nights a week so far, so if you hurry back you won't miss too many dinners," I told him.

He nodded. "Sounds like a plan, though unfortunately I'll be gone until a week from Tuesday." He looked across the table at Kay. "Kay, where's Ed these days? He should be here sharing this feast."

A little silence developed. At least now Kay knew I didn't spend my time with Bob talking about her on-again, off-again relationship with the chief of Willow Falls' little police department.

Kay looked frosty. "Ed who?" she asked.

"Uh oh," Bob said. "What went wrong this time?"

"I simply do not think it's appropriate for a police officer to laugh at the victim of a crime," she said.

Bob looked alarmed. "What happened?"

Kay sighed heavily. "I got conned with some fake traveler's checks. Well, you saw them, Louisa, didn't they look real to you?"

I nodded. I hadn't been there when Kay had taken the checks, but I saw them later. I would have had no hesitation in accepting them.

"So when I found out they were no good and reported it to my local police, they were uncooperative and rude," she said, and took another bite of her dinner. Bob waited while she chewed, then said, "Don't keep me in suspense, Kay."

She made a face. "Well, it was this woman. I kind of remember her, she was medium height and rather fat, maybe in her sixties, and she had these wild eyebrows. It was the eyebrows that did it. I just couldn't help looking at them, and then I didn't want to seem to be staring so I looked away, and she signed the traveler's checks in front of me and picked up her package and left."

"What did she buy?" he asked. "Obviously not a piece of furniture."

Kay and I looked at each other. She sighed and said, "Just the last piece of Louisa's mother's porcelain. It was a figure of Pan playing his pipes, with holes in the rock he sits on that you would put flowers in. The whole thing would be placed in a bowl of water."

Bob shook his head. "Doesn't ring any bells, but it doesn't sound like my kind of antique. Was it hideously valuable?"

She shook her head. "Not hideously. I had it marked at $500 because there was a tiny chip on the bottom, and this woman paid for it with hundred dollar traveler's checks. Well, I thought she paid," she added ruefully.

I remembered the day the Pan figurine got chipped. I was eight years old, sitting in the middle of my bed playing with some toys, a couple of little cars and a china horse, making up a story that involved them all. I decided to use the Pan for a mountain in the middle of the scene. I went to the living room to get it out of the china cabinet.

Pan was on a middle shelf. I lifted him down carefully, but not carefully enough and managed to clunk him against the corner of the cabinet. A small piece broke off the bottom of the rock on which he sat. I stared at that chip for what seemed like an eternity before I silently replaced him on his shelf. I picked up the little piece of porcelain from the floor, and hurried back to my room, feeling very guilty. I was afraid to tell my mother, but she didn't notice the chip for years. By the time she did I had learned that life went on even when you damaged porcelain Pans. I never confessed to the deed. Even Kay was unaware that I was the one who had lowered its value all those years ago.

Bob spoke again. "But where does Ed come into it?"

Kay wrinkled her nose. "He came by the store just after I'd found out the checks were fake, so I told him about it. First he started making jokes—"

"What she said was, Louisa's Pan has been stolen," I interjected, "which naturally provoked wisecracks about when did this become a kitchenware store, and how was I cooking without my pan."

Bob's lips twitched. "Naturally."

Kay went on. "Then when we got past his junior high humor and I told him about the traveler's checks, he started yelling at me because I hadn't attended his talk at the Chamber of Commerce a couple of weeks earlier when he had discussed this subject. So now it was all my fault that the perp was still at large. Which was completely unfair because even though I wasn't at the Chamber meeting I heard about his talk, and he hadn't said anything about eyebrows. I'm not at all sure it was the same person as the earlier incidents here and in High Cross. I don't appreciate being blamed for something that's not my fault. And I don't care to be yelled at in my own store. So I shoved him out the door and we haven't spoken since."

I sighed. I had come to like Ed, but he and my cousin were a volatile combination that was sometimes wearying to be around. Bob heard me and surreptitiously gave my hand a little squeeze under the table.

Just then Cleta came by the table again and looked at our plates. "Too bad none of you liked your dinners," she commented. All three plates were practically shiny clean.

"Does this mean we can have dessert, Miss Cleta?" Bob asked as she gathered the plates.

"You can have your own dessert," she agreed, "but Kay and Louisa have to share one."

"But I want my own!" Kay protested.

Cleta shook her head. "No, ma'am. I've noticed if you have something sweet in the evening then you grind your teeth in your sleep all night. The noise is awful. Louisa probably does the same thing. It's for your own good, young lady."

61

"Then just bring us the biggest dessert you've got," I told her.

7

"Bunny Farm Inn, may I help you?" I said into the kitchen phone.

"Oh, yes, hello, is this Miss Haskell?" asked a woman's voice.

"No, I'm sorry, Miss Haskell is not available. May I help you?"

There was a short silence, then, "This is Georgina Mason. We have a reservation for this weekend."

Hope blossomed. Maybe they weren't coming. "Yes, Miss Mason, we're expecting you today. Have your plans changed?"

"Oh, no. I'm calling to say that we've just passed Miller's Crossroads. We'll be there in twenty minutes or so."

Damn. "How nice of you to call. I'll meet you at the parking area. Do you have much luggage?"

There were some clicks and a sudden hollow sound on the phone, and then her voice came back. "—

suitcase for each of us, and of course we have our sweet little Rollo's things."

Mary Pat had warned me about sweet little Rollo. "Fine. I'll meet you in a few minutes.

Emily Ann and Jack were lying near the stove. When I reached for the coat hanging on the back of a chair they both jumped up wagging. "Sorry, guys, not this time. You guard the house and I'll be back in a few minutes with two ladies and another dog. Won't that be fun?"

Jack wagged enthusiastically, but Emily Ann gave me a skeptical look. I'm sure she could see through my bright tone. Since I'd come back to Willow Falls, my interactions with people—except for Bob and Kay and Ambrose—had mostly been brief and on the surface. Pleasant exchanges with shoppers in Kay's store, conversations about our pets at the dog park, a chat now and then with people at the Bluebird. I'd spent years doing personnel work, and after dealing with the tears and tangles and recriminations that occur in a busy workplace, this detachment had been incredibly restful. Being nice to the strangers who came to this inn would take more energy than I was now accustomed to expending on people.

When I went outside, though, it was a beautiful afternoon, and I felt my spirits lift. The cold air was crisp and pure, and the wintery blue of the sky was reflected in the lake. The bare trees were a lacy tangle against that blueness. I hummed as I climbed into the little station wagon that lived on the island.

Halfway down the drive I realized I should have asked them to meet me on this side of the bridge so I wouldn't have to walk on the damned thing. I'd already braved it that day to go out with Earlene and come back again. The house we'd gone to see had been a tired sixties rancher in the same tract where Emily Ann and Jack and I had gotten utterly lost as we fled on foot from the murderer we'd ultimately put in jail. Even if the house had been more interesting, I didn't want to live where the streets were so similar I'd never find my way home.

Now I was in luck, though. The Misses Mason and Gray had arrived and were halfway across the floating bridge. Each was pulling a medium sized suitcase on wheels. The one in the lead had a large lumpy knapsack slung over one shoulder, and her companion carried a mid-sized ice chest. In front of them ran a small dog, Toto to the life. I wondered how often they had to endure people commenting that he wasn't in Kansas anymore.

As soon as he saw me the dog began to bark. Actually, yap would be more accurate. He charged toward me, stopped a couple of feet away, and threatened me with annihilation. He was definitely the dog that Mary Pat had described earlier.

"Maybe it's the Toto thing," she'd told me during our training session. "I always expect Cairns to be polite and pleasant at the very least, but Rollo apparently didn't see the movie at an impressionable age. He fawns over his owners as long as they have food in their hands. He barks at strangers like he wants to kill them, and once he gets to know someone he's completely indifferent to them." She shook her head and her curls bounced. "But I have to say, for

65

some reason the little guy took to me right away. Maybe I smell like his mother, who knows."

Obviously Rollo was not mistaking me for Mary Pat.

"Don't worry, he won't hurt you," called one of the women, "he does that with everyone." She was tall and athletic looking, probably in her early thirties, with chin-length, silky brown hair in one of those cuts that fall perfectly into place whenever she moved her head. The kind of hair envied by those of us who struggle with humidity and gray hairs that are a completely different texture from everything else on our heads. But she also had a wide smile that was instantly likeable.

They stepped off the bridge and hurried toward me and Rollo. He whirled and started barking at them.

"Yeah, I can see he does." I had to raise my voice to be heard over his barking. How glad I was to hang out with Jack and Emily Ann. They didn't treat me like a stranger and they had deep voices that, while loud, were mercifully lacking in this fingernails-on-chalkboard quality.

"Rollo, sweetie, hush now," begged the other woman over the din the little dog was making. "Be quiet, that's a good boy." Rollo barked louder.

I raised my hand to straighten my glasses, and the movement made him spin back to bark at me. I reached in the pocket of my coat, found one of the dog treats that are usually there, and tossed it in his direction. He barked at it. I would tire of this soon. Then something behind me caught his attention. He stopped barking and stood at full, quivering attention.

I looked in the direction of his gaze and was startled to see Emily Ann and Jack trotting toward us.

They must have discovered the dog doors in the kitchen and followed me. There was a large one, and next to it a much smaller one, perhaps originally intended for cats. As far as I knew neither dog had used one before, but both had early lives that we knew little about. So either could have been trained to push through a flap. I thought the doors were locked, but evidently not—or one of my dogs knew how to pick locks. In any case, here they were, loping toward us.

After that first moment of silence, Rollo took a deep breath and began barking harder than ever, bouncing off his little front feet with every yap. The tall woman dropped the handle of her suitcase and the pack off her shoulder and darted toward him, trying to pick him up. But he eluded her and ran at my dogs.

I sucked in my breath as I watched a mental film in which Rollo attacked Jack or Emily Ann. Dogs don't pay much attention to size, and Rollo was not the type to acknowledge that the others were about ten times bigger than him. My mental camera panned in as the larger dog grabbed the terrier by the scruff of his neck and gave him a shake that stopped his barking permanently. This was followed by a scene in court where I pleaded with the judge that it had been justifiable homicide. Then a jail door was locked forever on me and Jack and Emily Ann. Some quick epilogue scenes showed Mary Pat losing her home and living out her twilight years on the streets with her possessions in a shopping cart.

I blinked my way back to reality. Rollo charged up to Jack, who waved his tail amiably. Emily Ann kept going, aiming for me. Rollo gave a final volley of barks at Jack before flinging himself at my greyhound. She paused to stare down her long, thin nose at him, then raised her head to gaze at the sky, clearly intending to have nothing to do with this fur-covered noise. Rollo fell on his back at her feet in total submission. Jack wagged some more and gave Rollo a sniff, but Emily Ann kept her nose raised, stepped over Rollo, and made her unhurried way to my side, where she sat down. Rollo bounced to his feet and ran in circles around us three or four times before falling down in front of Emily Ann again, wagging madly.

I struggled not to laugh, since his owners' faces were serious. "I think he's in love," the taller one said, and her companion nodded.

"It's perfectly understandable," I told them, "though I'm afraid his feelings may not be returned. But welcome to the Bunny Farm Inn."

I loaded their suitcases and bags into the back of the station wagon and slammed the hatch closed. When I turned, I found they had sorted themselves into the car. The tall woman—Miss Mason—was in the front passenger seat with Rollo on her lap. He had his paws on her shoulder and was straining toward Emily Ann, who was crowded into the back with Jack and Miss Gray. She had Jack partly over her lap. He looked very happy as she crooned to him and played with his big bassety ears.

The not-very-large car looked very full. As I got into the driver's seat and started the engine I felt more like a circus clown about to drive into the ring than a dignified innkeeper.

Soon we were in the foyer stripping off coats. "Go on into Mary Pat's office," I told them, knowing they'd been there several times before. "I'll be there in a moment to get you registered." I called Jack and Emily Ann and hurried with them to the kitchen. I threw my coat over a chair and then closed the door on the dogs so I could get the guests settled without Rollo getting in Emily Ann's way.

Back in the front of the house, I found the two women and their dog still standing in the hall. Miss Mason was looking at a watercolor of the lake, and turned to me and said, "Is this a new painting?"

I shrugged. "I don't think so. Mary Pat said her grandfather painted some of these things. But I don't know for sure. Shall we get you registered?"

They nodded and followed me past the stairway and down the little hall to the small room under the stairs that was Mary Pat's office. It was both businesslike and cozy. She had the usual desk and filing cabinets and computer, but the furniture was all warm oak, and the computer monitor had a custom-made dust cover of dark blue linen. The same linen upholstered the chairs. An old library table next to the desk held what was needed to register guests.

While Miss Mason filled in their form, Rollo dashed around the room, pausing occasionally to sniff something and then bark at it. Whenever I moved for any reason he would whirl and bark at me. When Miss Gray reached for her purse to get her credit card, he decided she needed to be barked at.

"Mary Pat said to put you in your usual room, so that's what I've done," I told them, raising my voice once more over Rollo's. "You can go on up."

"Oh," said Miss Gray, "wonderful."

There was a pause between the two words that puzzled me. "Would you prefer another room?" I asked. "The selection this time of year is pretty broad."

"Oh, no, that's definitely our favorite," Miss Mason put in quickly. "Could you help us carry one of these bags? Thanks. After you."

I took the knapsack she handed me and lead the way up the stairs. Mary Pat had said they always had the front room on the left. Throwing open the door, I let them precede me inside. I followed and placed the knapsack on the table in the corner of the room. "Anything I can get to help you settle in?" I asked, turning to look at them. They were both looking around the room as they set their bags down. "Everything okay?"

"Oh yes, fine," said Miss Mason. "We always enjoy this room so much." Her companion nodded.

"Okay, I'll leave you to get settled. Would you like me to make you a dinner reservation anywhere for this evening?"

Carolyn Gray shook her head. "No, we've taken care of dinner for tonight. But thanks. We'll unpack and then take Rollo out for a run."

I left them lifting suitcases onto the bed. Rollo barked me to the door. I was glad to shut it in his little yapping face.

It was about 9:30 that night when the phone rang. I was reading in bed, and reached over to pick up the extension on the night table. "Bunny Farm Inn, may I help you?"

"Hey, you actually answered the phone!" my cousin's voice came down the line.

"I am here in a professional capacity," I replied in dignified tones, "and as such I answer the phone." Dignity can only last so long. "So what's up?"

"Just wanted to check on you, and see if your first guests arrived."

"Them, and their little dog too," I told her. "So far so good, except that their dog barks at everyone, including them, and has fallen in love with Emily Ann."

"Emily Ann has a boyfriend?" she asked. "What does Jack think about that?"

"Since the boyfriend, as you put it, weighs only fourteen pounds, I don't think either of them is taking him too seriously. He is cute though, and he did finally stop barking at all of us."

"Did they just get him or something? Aren't terriers usually really loyal to their owners?"

"No, they've had him a while, because Mary Pat said they bring him out here each year for his birthday. Maybe it was just the excitement. They spent all afternoon letting him roam around the woods on the island and wore him out." The little guy was a pathetic sight when they brought him in at dusk. Miss Mason was cradling him in her arms, his short legs sticking up in the air and tongue lolling. He hadn't been able to summon the energy to bark any more.

"He's exhausted us all," she had told me. "Do you mind if we picnic in our room? We brought some goodies with us for dinner."

"No problem," I told her. "Use the microwave in the kitchen if you need it, and there's ice in the freezer."

She gave me a friendly smile. "Oh, we're pretty self sufficient. Carolyn planned this weekend, so that means all the details are taken care of." The two of them exchanged a fond glance before heading upstairs to their room.

"So you got your first guests checked in and taken care of?" Kay asked me now.

"It went just fine," I assured her. "They seem very nice, and not particularly demanding. If the other couple that's coming tomorrow is as pleasant I'll have it made."

"Well, if they want to pay with traveler's checks, be careful," she told me. "Cleta told me today that she heard about some other places that have taken bogus ones. The shop around the corner that sells those high-end house linens, and some restaurants here and in High Cross."

"Was it the same woman each time?" I knew her description had gone out to the other merchants in the area.

"No, it's been several different people. Well, probably. You know how bad most people are at describing someone they've seen for just a few minutes. But Cleta said that the ages were different, and it wasn't always a woman."

"Wow, maybe there's a ring of counterfeiters operating around here," I said. "Shades of the Hardy Boys."

"Yeah, well, the Hardy Boys grew up and became Ed, and who knows if he'll ever catch them. I just had a thought, though..." Her voice trailed off.

"What?" I prompted.

"Well, the one thing that's been consistent in the descriptions I've heard is that these people are all pretty heavy. I wonder if it could be a family that's doing it?"

"Mom and Dad teaching a trade to their offspring?" I thought about it for a moment. "Well, weirder things have happened."

"More like Grandma and Grandpa," she corrected. "The age range seems to be pretty broad."

"Maybe it's genetic, then. You always hear that some traits skip a generation."

She laughed. "True. Or maybe grandpa had to wait until the kid with the computer skills to do this got old enough to corrupt. They'll get caught one of these days, but I doubt we'll ever get the money for your porcelain Pan."

"Oh, who cares. It was just something of my mother's that I never liked."

"It irks me to get taken like that. I feel like I've cheated you."

"Make it up to me by coming out for dinner this weekend and keeping me company. Saturday."

"Okay, sounds good. What time?"

"Come out when you close the store."

"Oh, wait," she said. "Ambrose is coming over for dinner on Saturday."

"Bring him along," I told her. "He got me into this place, he can entertain me. How about Ed? Are you speaking yet?"

"Nope, not now, probably not ever."

I didn't believe that, but I knew better than to say so. "Fine, you and Ambrose for dinner."

"You want me to bring anything?"

"Can you throw together a salad? I'll make lasagna and fresh bread."

"Check. And I'll get Ambrose to bring some wine. This will be fun."

"If Ambrose is bringing the wine, it certainly will be," I agreed. I knew the kind of wine he bought and they didn't stock it at the Piggly Wiggly. "Okay, see you Saturday, cuz."

"Saturday," she said, and clicked off.

I put the phone back in its cradle and had just picked up my book when it rang again. Kay must have forgotten to tell me something. "Yeah, what did you forget?" I said into the receiver.

The silence that followed this had a startled quality to it, then Bob's voice said, "Well, you for one thing. I meant to pack you into my luggage and bring you along."

"Oh, Bob, sorry," I laughed. "I was just talking to Kay and figured she had called back."

"Yes, the phone was busy when I tried a little while ago. I got back from dinner with some colleagues and I wanted to call before you fell asleep."

He knows I keep early hours. "Are you having fun? How's the conference going?"

"No fun at all."

One of the great things about Bob is his knack for saying what you most want to hear.

"It's okay if you have a little fun," I told him. "It would be a shame to waste a week having no fun at all in San Francisco. I know, you can have a little practice fun on this trip, and we'll go back there together some time."

He laughed. "In that case, I guess I'm having just a small amount of fun. We had dinner at a South African restaurant this evening. There are restaurants everywhere here, every kind you can think of and then some."

"Was it better than the Bluebird?" I wanted to know.

His answer was immediate. "Not a bit."

"I'll tell Cleta and Dorothy," I told him. "Unless it might make them want to move to a big city somewhere and get rich and famous."

"Even if they wanted to, no one in Willow Falls would allow them to leave. But tell me how it's going with the inn?"

I assured him all was well, and we had a few more minutes of talk that verged on the mushy. We finally said good night and hung up. I heaved a deep sigh as I settled back against the pillows again, and reached for my book. The phone rang yet again. Kay? Bob? I was taking no chances this time.

"Bunny Farm Inn, may I help you?"

"Louisa! How are you?"

I hate it when people don't immediately identify themselves. I can rarely recognize any but my nearest and dearest. "Um, yes?"

"It's Mary Pat!" the voice went on.

"Mary Pat, hi," I said. "How is the trip? What time is it there?"

"Oh, it's the middle of the night." She sounded a little drunk. "A bunch of us were making the rounds of the local pubs, and then someone at the last pub suggested that the moors by moonlight were a sight we shouldn't miss, so we just got back from that."

There were muffled background noises that made me think she might still be in a pub.

"And were they?" I asked.

"Were what?"

"A sight not to be missed."

"I'll never know," she said, and giggled. "We couldn't find any moors in the dark."

"Ah." She sounded far more than a little drunk. I had never pictured Mary Pat this way.

"I thought I should call to make sure everything's okay on your end. Is everything okay on your end?"

"Everything's fine," I assured her. "Miss Mason and Miss Gray arrived today, and I'm all set for tomorrow's couple."

"That's wonderful. I knew you'd be wonderful. Oh, I just remembered. I called because I forgot to tell you something. I told Terry that you wouldn't need any help until this weekend. I said to come on Friday. Just don't let Terry mess with the computer, you know how kids love them."

76

As a matter of fact she had told me all this, but it seemed churlish to mention it. "Okay. Terry on Friday, no computer. Check."

"I have to go. I think I've woken everyone up here. Goodbye, goodbye." The phone went dead in my ear.

"Goodbye," I said to the dial tone, and hung up for a third time. I kept my hand over the receiver until I was fairly certain it wouldn't ring again. I thought fondly and a little sadly of my trusty answering machine that so faithfully screened phone calls for me, now packed in a box and locked up in a warehouse.

8

Perhaps from the exhaustion of answering the phone three times in a row, I had no trouble falling asleep on Thursday night. Darkness still cloaked the sky when I rose the next morning. I mixed biscuits ready to bake, and set out the dry breakfast comestibles in the dining room. I would add hot biscuits, yogurt and other dairy products, and fresh juice when the guests were ready to eat.

That done, I fed my dogs and slipped on my jacket to take them outside. Though both would probably have been fine on their own, they have hunting genes and I didn't want to worry about them if they took off after a rabbit or squirrel. It certainly was a luxury to know that there were no cars on the island to be a threat to them.

I perched on the teak bench under a big tree that in summer would be a comfortably shady spot, watching the dogs and thinking about the weekend ahead. I needed a few groceries for the lasagna I would serve Kay and Ambrose tomorrow night, but other than that my schedule for today was clear. I looked forward to having Terry arrive later to make the beds and clean bathrooms. The house was generally clean and well ordered and it wouldn't need much attention. I would see that the Misses Mason and Gray were fed this morning, and then I intended to give the dogs a long romp around the island. That other couple would arrive in late afternoon. Their plane was due into the High Cross airport about three o'clock. Getting them checked in would be child's play, since they wouldn't have Rollo helping them.

The thought of the terrier seemed to conjure up the real thing. I heard Rollo's bark and looked up to see him bounding toward me. Miss Gray followed, waving. Emily Ann and Jack came running, and the three dogs swirled around each other for a few moments as the woman came and sat beside me on my bench.

"Good morning," I said. "You're an early riser. I hope we didn't wake you."

She shook her head. "I always wake up early. There's no point trying to sleep any longer, so I take morning duties with Rollo. I hope his barking doesn't wake your other guests."

"No one else is here yet, but a couple is coming this afternoon."

"Are they bringing a dog too?" she asked.

"Not that I know of. Mary Pat said that about half her guests bring their dogs, so that would make us right on track statistically."

"We were sorry to miss Mary Pat this year," Miss Gray said. "Where did you say she went?"

"I don't think I said," I replied, wondering if it was some breach of innkeeper protocol to tell her. What the hell. "She's on a tour of B and B's in England with an innkeeper's association."

Carolyn Gray nodded. "Oh, that's right. She's told us about some of her trips. They go to a different country each year. She said she always comes back with lots of ideas from other small inns and hotels. Plus I think she really likes to shop."

"I don't know her very well," I admitted, "but having seen the house I would guess that, yes, she likes to shop."

"She always shows us her latest acquisitions when we stay here. I guess she must plan this trip for months."

"It was pretty last minute this year. She sent in her registration later than usual and got put on a waiting list, and only found out at the eleventh hour that she could go."

The romping dogs charged our way. Rollo was running full speed in front of the other two and looking back over his shoulder. I tried to move my legs out of his way, but I wasn't fast enough. He plowed into me. A small yelp came from each of us. Rollo bounced off and rolled over on his back. Jack came to stand between us.

"Are you okay?" Miss Gray asked.

"Sure," I told her. "This stuff happens at the dog park all the time. I'm just glad it was the smallest dog that hit me. I got plowed into by a sixty pound pit bull a couple of weeks ago and landed about five feet from where I'd been standing."

I had not been happy about the incident, or about the dog's owner telling me that her Phoebe only did that to people she liked. I may have bared my teeth at the woman as Scott, another of the dog park regulars, helped me back to my feet. Getting hit by Rollo was like being pummeled by a marshmallow in comparison.

"Well, I'm really sorry," Miss Gray said. "He should have better manners than to run into you."

Rollo had recovered by now and dashed off. After looking up into my face to make sure I was all right, Jack followed.

"Not to worry." I thought there were other areas in which Rollo needed better manners. "Is your friend up yet? Would you like some breakfast?"

"Oh, she'll be asleep for at least another hour. I thought I'd take Rollo for a walk. Would you and your dogs like to come along?"

Rollo was now barking alternately at Jack and Emily Ann. For such a small dog he had powerful lungs.

"Thanks, but I'll take them out later. I have some things I need to do now."

"Oh, don't go yet," she said quickly. "It's such a nice morning. I don't want to feel I've run you off."

"You haven't, not at all," I assured her. "I only came out to give these two their after-breakfast walkies. We were about to go in. Let me know when you're ready for breakfast." I rose and whistled, and Jack and Emily Ann came running. We started toward the back door of the inn. Halfway there I looked over my shoulder, intending to wave to Miss Gray, and was startled by the narrowed eyes and frown on her face. "What's the matter with her?" I muttered to the dogs, as we went through the back door into the kitchen. "She can't have wanted our company that much. Unless it was you guys she wanted, to play with Rollo."

Emily Ann gave an elegant snort.

"Now, now, you have to be nice to him," I told them. "After all, he is company." It was hard to put any conviction into my voice.

I took off my coat and draped it over a chair. If Miss Mason would be in bed for a while longer, I would have time to open and sort the mail that had come since Mary Pat left. Most of it would be junk, but she wanted me to go through it in case there were requests for reservations or bills that needed paying right away.

"Come on, guys, let's go to Mary Pat's office," I said. Jack rushed ahead into the hall and snuffled at the closed office door. I turned the knob and opened the door. Both dogs pushed in before me.

"Oh!"

I jumped at the startled exclamation. Miss Mason stood by the desk. She wore a pink quilted bathrobe and fuzzy slippers, and as I looked at her, her cheeks flooded with matching pink.

"What are you doing in here?" I was too surprised to sound more tactful.

"I think I left my credit card in here yesterday when we were registering," she said. "When I saw I didn't have it I wanted to find it right away."

"It's not here. I remember you putting it back in your purse," I told her. "You dropped your bag and Rollo barked at you."

Her expression cleared. "Oh, that's right. Maybe I put it in the wrong part of my wallet. I'll look again. Thanks. Have you seen Carolyn anywhere?"

"Yes, she's outside with your dog."

"Oh, good. I'll get dressed and join her."

"When would you like breakfast?"

"Um, would an hour be all right? That will give me time to shower and stretch my legs."

"Fine. I'll have everything ready in the dining room." I could feel the stony expression on my face, but it was the best I could do.

"Thanks. And I'm sorry I startled you. I was just worried about my card. We're planning to go antiquing while we're here and I'd hate to find the perfect piece and not be able to buy it."

She turned and left the room. Jack followed her to the door and into the hall, then came back and stuck his nose in my hand.

I reached out and pulled the door shut. "We'd better look around and make sure everything's okay," I told the dogs.

I scanned the room from where I stood and couldn't see anything out of place. I went over to the desk. Papers seemed to be where they had been the last time I looked.

Maybe she really had been looking for her credit card.

Maybe.

Then I remembered it hadn't been Miss Mason who had given me her card. I was sure it had been Miss Gray. I frowned as I looked around again, but I could see nothing wrong. Maybe listening to Rollo's constant barking had addled the two of them. And Mary Pat had said they were schoolteachers; daily doses of clamoring children might have the same effect (and would certainly explain why the barking of one small dog didn't disturb them).

I decided to get the two women fed and off on their day's adventures, then come back and check the office more methodically.

I led the dogs into the hall and pulled the door closed after us. I took a step toward the kitchen, then stopped and turned back. What was it they would do in the old spy movies so they would know if their hotel room had been entered while they were out skulking about? Oh, they'd stretch a hair from the door knob across the crack of the door and check to make sure it was still in place when they came back.

I looked around to make sure I was unobserved, then reached up and yanked a hair out of the top of my head. I looked at what I had reaped. It was about three inches long and it was one of the gray ones. I shrugged and laid the hair over the door knob. I could see no way to drape it across the intersection with the door frame, because the metal plate that the latch went into protruded slightly on the inside of the door, not the outside. Maybe the idea was that you just left it on the door knob itself and if anyone turned it, the hair would fall to the floor. But as soon as I removed my fingers, down it went.

I bent over to pick it up and encountered the steady gazes of Jack and Emily Ann, sitting side by side about a foot away. They stared at me with interest.

"It's nothing," I told them, straightening up and leaving the hair on the floor. "Just wanted to try something. Come on, let's go to the kitchen."

I thought they gave each other a conspiratorial look as I turned, but they followed me as they always do. I pushed open the swinging door. The phone began to ring.

I made sure the dogs were through the door before I let go and crossed the room to where the phone sat on a little table. "Good morning, Bunny Farm Inn," I caroled into the mouthpiece.

"Um, hello?" It was a young voice.

"Yes, hello?" I encouraged.

"Um, well, is this Mrs. McGuire?"

"Yes it is."

"Um, well, this is Terry? I'm the one who works for Mary Pat? I help her with the housework?"

"Oh, yes, Terry. I'm looking forward to meeting you. I understand you're scheduled to come in at two this afternoon for a few hours, right?" I hoped Miss Mason and Miss Gray didn't leave their bathroom too messy, since this young-sounding voice belonged to the person who was going to be cleaning up after them. Though my baser self felt strongly that anyone who inflected every sentence as a question deserved some sort of punishment.

"Um, well, see, I can't come then?"

85

"Do you mean you're going to be late? That's fine, just let me know what time to expect you." Good, I thought, if Terry is coming later I'll have more time to do the shopping.

"Um, no, well, I can't come at all?"

"What?"

"Well, see, I have the measles?"

I have taken dozens, perhaps hundreds of these phone calls over the years. Most were routine: I can't come to work because I'm sick. Occasionally you got a message that was too honest: I can't come to work because I'm too hung over to get out of bed. Or enigmatic: I can't come to work because I have something else to do today. Some were just gross; they didn't tell you they were sick, they lovingly enumerated their disgusting symptoms one by one— usually involving slime or mysterious swellings or unmentionable body parts. One person had called from the airport to say she was on her way to China to pick up a baby girl she was adopting. Another had called from Albuquerque because her car had broken down while she was on vacation and it was going to take her several days to sell it and get other transportation home. A man had lisped into my voice mail that he had lost the bridge which replaced his front teeth and he had to go to the dentist to get another. Countless people had been in minor car wrecks on their way to work and had to deal with the aftermath. Curiously enough some of their cars showed absolutely no damage the following day. Once I'd gotten a call from a hospital because a programmer at the software company I worked for had sleep-walked his way off a second floor balcony and broken several bones.

But no one had ever called me before because they had the measles.

"Terry, are you sure it's the measles? Couldn't it be just hives or some kind of allergic rash?"

"Um, well, my mom took me to the doctor, and like, she said it's, like, measles."

I was not happy to hear this, but relieved to finally have a statement and not a question.

"Oh. All right. Well, if you're sick, you're sick. Stay home and in bed and get well soon, and let me know when you think you can work again."

"I'm sorry I got sick," was the glum reply. "Um, Mrs. McGuire..."

"Yes, Terry?"

"Oh, nothing. I'll, like, call you when I'm better?"

"Fine, and I hope you're better soon."

I hung up the phone and looked at Jack and Emily Ann. "I'll pay you guys ten dollars an hour to clean the guest bathrooms," I told them. Jack stood up and grinned at me, confident that I was joking. Which just shows that dogs aren't psychic after all.

When I went into the dining room to pour coffee for their breakfast, Miss Mason smiled at me in a beseeching way. "I found my credit card. I tucked it into the place for bills instead of its usual pocket. I'm so glad you remembered seeing me put it in there."

"Oh. Good." I knew my voice was stiff. Should I remind her it had been her friend who used her credit card to register?

"Sorry about being in the office and startling you. We've stayed here so often I guess I feel too much at home."

I bent the corners of my mouth. "Not at all. I'm just glad you found your card. I know identity theft is always a worry these days."

She seized on that explanation. "Oh, that is so true. It happened to a friend of ours, and his credit was nearly ruined. It took months to straighten everything out."

"Very trying," I agreed. "I'll leave the coffee pot on the warmer here. Is there anything else you need?"

"No, this is wonderful," said Miss Gray. "A feast compared to what we usually have in the mornings."

I left them to return to the kitchen and my own breakfast. Just as I took a sip of tea, the phone rang. The quick part of my brain—the part that jumps to conclusions with no evidence for the leap—said it was Terry calling back; it wasn't the measles after all. Sometimes I impress myself with my ability to conjure hope out of nothing.

"Good morning, Bunny Farm Inn," I said into the receiver.

"You do that just beautifully," responded a warm voice. "Louisa, this is Mary Pat. How are you this morning?"

"Mary Pat, hello. I'm fine. Have you recovered from your pub crawl last night?"

"I beg your pardon?" Her tone was puzzled.

"I just meant that when you called last night you sounded—"

"What do you mean, when I called last night?"

Now it was my turn to be mystified. "You called me last night. You said you'd been out to some pubs and had gone looking for the moors but couldn't find them."

I had already experienced the warm, delightful Mary Pat, and the drunken Mary Pat. Now I found there was also a chilly Mary Pat. "Louisa, excuse me, but I did not call you last night. You must have fallen asleep and dreamed it."

"I don't think—" I hedged, but didn't get any further.

"Don't worry about it," she cut in. "I too sometimes have very realistic dreams." Perhaps she meant to sound kind, but it came across as patronizing. "I just wanted to see how you are doing. Did Rollo and his owners arrive all right?"

"Yes, they're here, but I found one of them in your office this morning."

"In my office, Louisa? Why would she be in my office?" She sounded almost as though she didn't believe me. Maybe she thought I'd dreamed this too.

"She said she thought she'd left her credit card when I checked them in, but—"

"That's something you'll need to be very careful of. Make certain you give people back their cards. If anyone sues you for keeping their credit card, I'm sorry but you'll be on your own. I certainly can't accept any liability for your actions."

"But—"

"That probably wouldn't happen with Miss Mason and Miss Gray. After all, they've known me for years. Oh, hold on a moment—"

She muffled the mouthpiece of her phone. I heard vague noises, and then she was back.

"Louisa, I have to go. We're getting ready to board our bus. I'll call you again in a day or so. Good bye."

The dial tone buzzed in my ear. I hung up the phone and glared at it. Who did she think she was? Who was doing whom the favor here? I looked over at Jack and Emily Ann, lying near the table.

"Do you guys think Mary Pat could be schizophrenic?" Jack cocked his head. "It means crazy," I told him. "Pretty much just means crazy."

9

The dishwasher settled into its grinding hum as I headed up the back stairs, bucket of cleaning supplies in one hand and rags in the other. The dogs were at my heels, but I detoured by my room to leave them there while I got the chores over with. If Terry wasn't coming this weekend, I wanted to get the cleaning done as soon as I could.

The heavy side door had closed behind my two guests and their dog a few minutes earlier. From the kitchen window, I'd seen them walking single file along the path that led to an old shed down by the lake. From there they could roam all over the island. Rollo investigated the base of a tree, then dashed after them, only to be seduced by another smell. Then he looked up, saw he was being left behind, barked, and ran to catch up.

I was still fuming over Mary Pat's phone call as I closed my bedroom door on the dogs. How dare she tell me I had imagined her phone call in the night? Not to mention that crack about not being responsible for my actions. I couldn't decide whether I should call my lawyer or start my new credit card collection with the very next person who checked in.

I headed around the corner and down the hall to the room the two women were occupying. I knew they were out, but I knocked before I opened their door and peeked in.

A quick look reassured me that they were not particularly messy guests. Mary Pat had carefully avoided telling any horror stories when she showed me the ropes. In fact she had made innkeeping sound so easy that I wondered why she didn't just let fifteen year old Terry run the place. But I knew that some people assume that having maid service in a hotel room means they can wreak as much havoc as they like.

Miss Mason and Miss Gray might go skulking about in other people's offices, but they had not created a great deal of disorder in their room. I felt better about them.

The bedcovers had been pulled up, and the pink bathrobe I'd seen earlier was tossed on top of the bed. I hung it in the closet and made the bed. The table in the corner showed evidence of their picnic dinner the night before. A couple of heavy paper plates and plastic wine glasses were stacked in the middle of the table, and there was a note on the inn's stationery beside some take out containers. "Hi—would you mind tossing these leftovers in the kitchen trash? Thanks!" I peeked into one of the containers. Looked like they had had a pesto-based potato salad as part of their feast. I'd have to try that sometime. I swept everything from the table into a trash can and set it by the door to take downstairs, then checked the tea paraphernalia. I looked around and decided the room looked fine. Now for the bathroom.

I honestly do not think I'm too good to clean up after other people. My reluctance to do the bathrooms stemmed from the same summer camp experience that formed my dread of bridges. (I've always thought that visiting a psychiatrist would be a waste of my time, because the genesis of my various quirks are perfectly easy to identify.)

After I'd taken to hiding in my friendly tree, Mrs. Mayhew, the camp's director, became more and more annoyed at my refusal to participate in camp activities. She called me sullen. She threatened to telephone my parents. I knew they were traveling in South America so I was unintimidated. I hoped she would call Kay's parents, because they might rescue me if they knew what kind of summer I was having. I kept hiding, and avoided the fun hikes through the woods, the rope bridge, the fireside ghost stories and other campy things.

My cabin mates were just as annoyed as Mrs. Mayhew. They simply could not figure out where I went to escape them. I was considered such a klutz that it simply didn't occur to them that I could climb a tree. I resolutely endured the teasing and taunts and tricks by pretending they did not exist, which I was gratified to see that they absolutely hated. And I hid in my leafy green world as often as possible. I smuggled up some books to read and a canteen of water, and while the experience would have been vastly improved with the addition of some chocolate, it was a great deal better than being nauseous on a swinging rope bridge.

Lisa and Jodi were sly but not stupid. They took note of Mrs. Mayhew's anger with me, and on the morning of one of our weekly cabin inspections, they went to work. When the camp director arrived, she found the two of them in tears.

"Oh, Mrs. Mayhew, we tried to stop her," Lisa hiccupped.

"Stop who, dear? Tell me what's wrong," Mrs. Mayhew said gently, putting an arm around each sobbing girl's shoulder.

Jodi appeared to be crying too hard to speak. "L-L-L-Louisa," she finally managed. I looked up from my bunk, where I was reading. Now what?

They led Mrs. Mayhew to the bathroom. She stopped in the doorway and gasped. I scrambled off my bunk and hurried to where she stood, peering around her. They had wrecked our bathroom. Rolls of toilet paper were stuffed the commodes, toothpaste (everyone's but mine) smeared every surface, shampoo glazed the floor. She turned slowly and glared at me.

"I have no idea what is the matter with you, young lady," she snarled, biting off each word, "but this kind of vandalism will absolutely not be tolerated."

I felt hot, then cold, and my throat closed so that I could hardly breathe. I cowered under her furious glare. She read my fear as guilt. "Get in there and clean up this mess. Until this bathroom is spotless, you are not to show yourself in the mess hall. I don't care if it takes you a week. Come, girls." She shepherded Lisa and Jodi out of the cabin. Jodi couldn't resist looking back over her shoulder and smiling.

"But—but I didn't do anything," I said to their retreating backs. If they heard me, it didn't matter.

I turned back to what I had to clean up if I ever wanted to eat again. Which I did, even if it was camp food. Since there was no one there to see me I slumped in the doorway and cried and cried.

Now, in the front left bedroom of the Bunny Farm Inn, I felt some of the same trepidation as I slowly pushed opened the door to the adjoining bath. I gave an audible sigh of relief at the sight of damp towels hung over towel bars, and personal toiletries corralled in wicker baskets.

Okay, so they had a dog that barked a lot and they made themselves free of rooms where they had no business being. Entering the bathroom to gather the used towels and wipe down the sink and counter, I thought to myself that so far, the virtues of Miss Mason and Miss Gray greatly outweighed their vices.

10

Once I installed fresh towels and refreshed the flower arrangement on the dresser, the room was done. I gathered up my supplies and the trash can and went back to my own room to let the dogs out. They were sleeping back to back on top of the bed. Emily Ann thumped her whippy tail on the comforter at the sight of me.

"Did you two have a nice nap?" I asked, though I knew Emily Ann considered all naps to be good ones. "Let's go back downstairs and make the shopping list so we can get our errands done. And I have to go back over the office and make sure everything is all right in there." They scrambled off the bed at the word "go" and preceded me down the back stairs. I stowed my cleaning supplies and settled at the table with a pen and pad of paper to consider what I needed for tomorrow night's dinner with Kay and Ambrose.

I jotted down half a dozen items before the phone rang. It occurred to me that you could tell whether you were working or not by how many times a day the phone rings. A lot of calls equal work, few calls equal regular life. Some people have busy social lives so they get many calls, but to me that seems like a type of work.

"Good morning, Bunny Farm Inn," I answered the phone.

"Ah, good morning." I wasn't sure if the voice was male or female, it occupied that middle ground where it could be either. "I was wondering if you have any rooms left for this weekend?"

Damn. Another guest. "What kind of accommodation do you need?"

"I'm looking for a single room until Monday."

I had been hoping the voice would need rooms for a party of twelve, which I could honestly have denied being able to handle. I couldn't find any excuse not to take in one more person. "That should be no problem. Would you like to hear about the rooms I have, or shall I just choose one for you?"

"Oh, you choose. All I require is a private bath, and as quiet a spot as possible. I am a light sleeper."

"I have just the thing for you. May I have your name, please?"

"Barton Potter."

That seemed to answer the male or female question, I thought, as I wrote down the name. "May I have your credit card number, Mr. Potter?"

He rattled off a string of numbers, which I jotted down, then repeated back to him. "And will you be bringing your dog with you?" I inquired.

There was a moment of silence. "My dog?"

97

"Yes, this inn allows dogs, so a number of people do bring their pets along."

"How delightful," he said. I couldn't tell if he meant it or not. "I'm afraid I don't have a dog myself. Perhaps I can enjoy the others that are there this weekend. Are there many?"

"Just three," I told him. "Do you need directions to the inn? Oh, and what time do you think you will be arriving?"

"Let me see," he said. A short silence while he calculated. "I'll arrive a bit late, sometime after six this evening. When do you serve dinner?"

"Sorry, we do breakfast only. Oh, and tea in the afternoon if you want it, though you will be arriving too late this evening for that, I'm afraid." Be firm, I told myself. With any luck he'll take a dislike to you and change his mind about coming here.

"And you couldn't make an exception? I'd really planned to settle in for the evening and won't want to go out again for dinner."

"I'm sorry, it's not possible. If you like I can suggest other inns closer to town. Or you could bring something with you and dine in your room." I started mentally running through the list of inns in Willow Falls where I could unload this guy.

"I suppose that's what I'll have to do." He gave a petulant sigh. "I need a complete get-away and your inn sounded like just the thing. Could you give me the directions from High Cross? I'll be coming through there."

I complied, then said, "We'll look for you this evening, then. If you have a cell phone you can call me

98

when you're getting near and I'll meet you at the bridge. Or there's a phone at the gas station in Miller's Crossroads, which you'll pass through."

"Thank you, I'll do that." And Mr. Potter hung up the phone.

I thought about where to put this new guest. The Oak Room seemed like just the thing, around a corner and down a hall from the other rooms currently occupied. Mary Pat's suite was across the hall. Since it was empty, the Oak Room should be the quiet haven Mr. Potter was seeking. It was also a manly sort of room, with a heavy iron mantel over the fireplace and oak wainscoting. The fireplace had a gas insert which burned cozily, safer and less messy for guests to use. The room would be perfect when I added fresh towels, tea things, and some flowers. I could raid the dining room arrangements for mums and other materials.

I could see my day, so unencumbered when I sat under the tree earlier, filling with necessary trivia. No doubt my shopping trip would take much longer than I expected too. I'd have to put off inspecting the office until I'd accomplished more pressing tasks. After all, Miss Mason couldn't have been in there very long, and everything had looked all right.

I completed my list and was bundling up to make the trip to town when the phone rang. Fighting down the urge to sigh as petulantly as Mr. Potter had done, I picked it up. "Good morning, Bunny Farm Inn."

"Louisa? Is that you?"

It was Earlene, and the fact that I recognized her voice must mean that she had become one of my nearest and dearest. I resolved to buy a house very soon.

"Yes, Earlene. What can I do for you?"

"Well, would you believe that I have just found out about a house for sale not too far from that place where you're staying?"

"Really? I don't know, Earlene, this is a lot further from town than I was thinking of moving."

This was not enough to deter Earlene. "Oh, I'm aware of that, dear, but you just never know. If you fell in love with this house you wouldn't mind the drive, and it's supposed to be a beautiful area. It won't hurt to take a look if you have time."

"I don't think I can today," I said, thinking of my to-do list.

"Well then, how about tomorrow?"

All the guests would have arrived, and my shopping would be done. If I was in the middle of making lasagna, it could be put on hold while I went out with Earlene. "Yes, that should work. About ten in the morning? Call me just before you get here and I'll meet you at the bridge."

"Wonderful. I'll see you then."

I hung up the phone, and turned to reach for my jacket. I wanted to get out of the house before another call came in, but then realized I should take the inn's cell phone with me. I scowled at the house phone as I programmed it to forward calls to the cell, as Mary Pat had shown me. Dropping the cell into my pocket felt exactly like putting a yoke around my neck.

11

A green light on the computer keyboard glowed. I turned on the monitor and the desktop swam into focus, a photo of the Bunny Farm Inn with a host of dogs lined up on the porch and in the yard. I wondered if all those dogs had really been there, or if the picture had been manufactured. Icons for several graphics programs shared the screen with the usual word processing, spreadsheet and database programs.

None of the programs were open. I am methodical about shutting down a computer, but I was out of my regular routine in this place. I couldn't swear that I had shut everything down the day before. But my uneasiness at finding Miss Mason in the office that morning was reignited. Yet I didn't see anything on the screen that I thought would be of interest to a schoolteacher from High Cross. I turned off the computer and began to search the room. In a few minutes I learned that my problem wasn't that anything was missing from the room. The problem was what was there.

I started with file drawers, ignoring the voices in my head. "She'll be furious if she finds out you searched her files," the scaredy cat said. My internal defender retorted, "Then she should have been nicer on the phone this morning. The woman is certifiable." I found receipts for paid bills, pull sheets for ads for the inn, letters. The bottom drawer held several packs of variously sized batteries and a digital camera. I wondered if she had more than one camera; I would have expected her to take one with her on her tour of England.

The office was built into the space under the staircase. Part of the ceiling slanted, and there were no windows. It was a snug little cave, made cozy by rows of books. Two of the office walls were lined with bookcases. Many of the volumes were from the early part of the last century, obscure novels as far as I could see. I wondered if they might be valuable first editions, though from their worn condition alone I would question any great value. I thought they had been purchased more with an eye to decorating than to literary quality. Or perhaps they had been in the house since her grandparents' time.

As I looked around at the shelves, I noticed something curious. On all but one bookcase, the tomes were pushed back two or three inches from the edge of the shelves, with small objects placed here and there in front of the books. A gold-plated police whistle, a wooden top stained blue with a red ribbon to spin it, an egg carved out of green-striped malachite.

But on the shelves in the right hand corner of the room, the books were all lined up precisely on the edge, like in a public library. I went over to look at the books, wondering if they were too long to be pushed back. I reached in over them and ran my hand along the backs to see if they touched the back of the case. One or two did, but most were the same general size as those shelved on the other cases.

Then, just as I was about to bring my hand back out and shrug off the difference in this one bookcase, I brushed against something hard. It was cool to the touch and irregularly shaped. Without being able to see it I couldn't figure out what it might be. So I pulled several volumes off the shelf and laid them on the desk, then went back and reached in to grab whatever was there.

The object I pulled out was porcelain, about twice the size of my fist: a Pan figure sitting on a rock, with small holes around it.

My first reaction was one of pleasure. "Hey, Emily Ann," I said. "Look at this. Mary Pat has a Pan figurine like the one we used to have. I wonder how many of them there are around." Emily Ann looked interested, as though this might be something a dog could eat.

Then I turned the figurine over, and saw the little chip on the bottom. The chip that I had put there all those years ago.

I'm afraid the first words out of my mouth were, "Holy shit." Both dogs came over and looked at me with inquiring expressions.

103

"It's my Pan," I told them. My voice shook just a little. "The one that was paid for with counterfeit traveler's checks."

Emily Ann lifted her long nose and gave the figurine a sniff. Too late I remembered that smells would not be the only thing on it, there could have been fingerprints too. Now they were underneath mine.

I took the Pan back to the desk and placed it next to the computer, then sank onto the blue linen upholstery of the chair. Had Mary Pat bought it from the woman who had used the fake checks? I knew from Kay's description of the thief that they couldn't be the same person. Mary Pat certainly didn't have eyebrows that would rivet your attention.

Then I remembered Kay's theory that it could be a family passing the bogus traveler's checks. Could Mary Pat be a member of the same family? She did have the same body type that Kay had described. Of course, Kay and I and half the women we knew could be part of that family as well.

I reached for the phone and dialed Kay's number. She had to hear about this right away.

"OKay Antiques," came her cheerful voice.

"Kay, it's me," I started.

"Oh, Louisa, let me call you back. I can't talk right now."

"But—" The phone was already dead.

Who else would know anything about Mary Pat? Ambrose, of course. I dialed his number.

"This is Ambrose," I heard after the third ring. From the background sounds I guessed he was in his car.

"Ambrose, it's Louisa," I said. "I have a question for you. Does Mary Pat have any sisters who live around here?"

"Sisters? No, she's an only child, and I remember her saying once that both her parents were too. We were talking about family traditions and she claimed that was one of theirs."

"So no cousins or anything."

"Not close ones. Why do you ask?"

Maybe I should have told him about the Pan. But I didn't. "Oh, I thought I saw someone at the grocery store who looked like her, and I just wondered."

"I see. No, she's one of a kind. Listen, I'm about to get on the freeway."

"Okay. Drive safely and I'll talk to you later." I hung up the phone. The Pan leered at me, I was sure of it.

"What the hell am I going to do with you?" I asked it. Just then I heard barking, and the slam of the side door. Miss Mason and Miss Gray were back with Rollo. Their laughing voices went past the closed office door, then I heard footsteps ascending the stairs. Could they have anything to do with the figurine? Could Miss Mason have been looking for it when she was in here earlier?

Or planting it behind the books?

I thought about putting it back where I had found it, and calling Ed to come and arrest it. If we had been in Willow Falls I might have done this, but we were out of Ed's jurisdiction here. Even though she'd been so rude on the phone, I was reluctant to bring the kind of trouble to Mary Pat that might result from calling the sheriff's office.

I picked up the Pan once more and frowned at him, then made up my mind. Setting him down again, I went over and replaced the books I had pulled off the shelf. I considered placing some other object behind them, thinking someone might reach back there and be reassured and not look at what they were touching. But I couldn't think of anything to use that would feel the same even to a casual touch. I decided to leave the space empty. I picked up the Pan and tucked it under my sweater, holding it in the crook of my elbow. I made sure it was covered, then slowly opened the office door and peeked out. No one was in sight.

As I opened the door further, Jack barreled through the opening, jerking the knob out of my hand and pushing me off balance. I steadied myself on the door jamb. Then I turned right to go upstairs, so I could hide the Pan somewhere in my room. I rounded the corner and put my foot on the first step. A voice spoke from the parlor a few feet away. Too late I realized that only one pair of feet had gone upstairs with Rollo.

"Mrs. McGuire, there you are," said Miss Mason. "I was hoping I'd catch you." She stood in the living room with a magazine in one hand. Jack leaned against her, wagging his tail. She bent down to give him a pat.

Traitor, I thought, giving Jack a look. I kept one foot on the step, hugging the Pan to my side. I hoped I was generally lumpy enough for a china figurine not to be noticeable under my sweater.

"Oh, Miss Mason, you startled me. What can I do for you?"

Her pink cheeks got a little pinker. "Sorry, didn't mean to be lying in wait. I have a favor to ask. We're planning to go out this evening, and I wondered if it would be all right to leave Rollo here while we're gone. We always do when Mary Pat is here, but I wanted to check with you. We could take him along, but it's pretty cold to leave him in the car while we have dinner."

"Of course. He can hang out with Jack and Emily Ann." The Pan was burning a hole in my ribs.

"He shouldn't be any trouble," she went on, relaxing now that I had said yes. "He's been running all over. Of course by this evening it may be just me and Carolyn who are tired. He seems to be inexhaustible."

"Well, maybe Emily Ann can persuade him to take a nap," I said. "It's her specialty. Would you excuse me? I need to—to check on something in the kitchen." It had occurred to me that if I went upstairs, with my luck I would undoubtedly run into Miss Gray as well.

"Of course. I didn't mean to keep you. We came back so Caro could change shoes. She got her feet wet and I don't want her to catch pneumonia. We'll be going out again in a few minutes."

"I'll be serving afternoon tea about 4:30 if you are interested," I said, taking my foot off the step and starting back down the hall. "Have a fun afternoon."

"That sounds great," she said. "Thanks."

I probably looked like I was nursing broken ribs as I walked stiffly away, holding that damned Pan against me. In the kitchen I took it out from under my sweater and held it up to eye level. Pan sat calmly on his china rock, playing his stupid flute.

"What was it you did, according to the Greeks or Romans or Etruscans or whoever it was?" I growled at him. "Created chaos? Well, knock it off."

I looked around, trying to figure out where to stash the thing. The upper cabinets all had open shelving, which didn't seem promising. I started to reach for a door to one of the lower cabinets, then stopped. I was afraid if I put the Pan in with the pots and pans and trays, he might get banged up while I was taking ironware in and out. I could just imagine Kay's face if I had to tell her I'd found the thing and then managed to break it. Then my eye landed on the Welsh dresser across the room, the one loaded with Mary Pat's collection of tea pots. All sizes and styles and colors and shapes of china pots. One more object in the already riotous mass would not be likely to draw attention. I'd hide Pan in plain sight, like ET among the closetful of stuffed toys.

"There," I said to Pan as I settled him behind several similarly colored pots. "You stay there until I figure out what to do with you, and don't go knocking the teapots off the shelf."

12

The afternoon sun sank into a nest of clouds as I waited for the expected couple to arrive. I ran the car engine to stay warm, but turned it off when I saw a white sedan pull into the parking area across the floating bridge.

The weather had grown increasingly cold and raw during the day, in spite of the wintry sunshine. A tang in the air warned of impending snow. I usually enjoy snow. We don't get so much that it's a burden. But by late February enough is enough. Climbing out of the little station wagon, I pulled on my gloves and wrapped the muffler one more turn around my neck, then waved to my next guests. The woman said something to the man, who nodded, then she started my way.

The next moment the peace of the winter afternoon was shattered.

"LEW-EEE-SA! MY GOD, IS THAT YOU?"

I stared in disbelief at the figure approaching over the floating bridge. It couldn't be...but it was. A nightmare in the flesh.

Doris.

"Good god, every time I come to this part of the country, there you are!" she shouted. She was not smiling. "What the hell are you doing here?"

She was now about three feet away but had not modulated her voice as she approached. I tried not to wince at the volume. Doris is tall and has excellent posture. She wears dramatic clothes and a very simple haircut. She is formidable.

"I'm minding the Bunny Farm while the owner is in England," I told her. "More to the point, what are *you* doing here? I live around here and you live in Seattle, so it's far more peculiar for you to show up."

I felt a secret glow of pride as I listened to myself. For too many years I would never have answered her like that. Doris was one of my late husband's partners in his law firm, and I had always found her terrifying. When I wasn't able to avoid her she reduced me to tongue-tied insipidity with her complete lack of tact or sensitivity. But facing down the gun of a two-time murderer intent on adding you to his list can be a life-altering experience in many ways. I was no longer so afraid of mere words.

Her companion had followed her across the bridge. He was about the same height as Doris, a couple of inches taller than me, and his stocky body sported powerful-looking shoulders under his calf-length black wool coat. He carried a mid-sized suitcase in each hand as casually as Doris handled her purse. Setting them down a few feet away, he approached me with his hand out.

"Good afternoon," he said, giving me a dazzling view of white teeth. "I'm William Jones."

His hand was warm despite being gloveless in the frosty air. As soon as he released our handshake, Doris reached over and grabbed his hand and held it.

"Louisa, this is my husband," she said, looking at him and lingering over the last word. I waited for her to complete the introduction but apparently she was finished.

"Louisa McGuire," I supplied. "Goodness, Doris, I had no idea you had married." To Mr. Jones I added, "My late husband and Doris worked together."

"It only happened this week. We're on our honeymoon."

The two of them smiled stupid smiles at each other. Neither seemed to feel the blast of icy wind off the lake. Maybe if Bob had been there I wouldn't have noticed it either, but under the circumstances I was starting to feel like a block of ice.

"Well. Congratulations, both of you, I hope you'll be very happy. Shall we head up to the house? Is there more luggage in your car? We can take a cart down to get it."

He unlocked his gaze from hers and turned back to me. "There are a couple more cases, but I can bring them up later. Let me just get these two and we can go."

He detached himself from Doris's grip and turned back to the two cases. Her eyes never left him. I'd

111

better be careful if I sent them out for a walk while they were here. Doris would have herself in the lake. And in this weather she'd freeze to death in no time. Oh darn, I thought maliciously, wouldn't that be a pity.

Miss Mason and Miss Gray were playing checkers at the game table near the fire in the small sitting room when I rolled in the cart for tea. Emily Ann had arranged herself on the settee, and Rollo lay below her on the floor. He blinked at me wearily as I entered. The two women had exercised him into oblivion. There's a saying among dog owners that a tired dog is a good dog, and Rollo was living proof. Jack was at my heels. He liked to help in the kitchen.

The winter afternoon was already nearly dark, and a couple of lamps were lit, making the whole scene almost unbearably cozy.

Doris walked in.

Rollo raised his head and opened his mouth to bark, then flopped down again. I looked at him in alarm. This was taking tired-out to the extreme. Rollo not barking seemed unnatural. Maybe they had drugged his dinner.

"Oh, good, tea," Doris said. Game players and dogs turned their heads to look at her. She didn't notice. Grabbing the newspaper off my favorite chair, she sat down and settled back. "I'm exhausted, it's been a long day. Have you noticed how much worse air travel is getting? Even first class is always full and there's all that waiting and waiting and waiting. Not to mention getting through security. Of course they never search *me*."

She peered at the headlines on the paper in her hand and then dropped it on the floor.

"Miss Mason, Miss Gray, may I introduce you to Mrs. Jones?" I said. Their eyes were fixed on her like birds confronted with a snake. Both mumbled something inarticulate. "Miss Mason and Miss Gray bring Rollo to stay here every year on his birthday," I forged on. "Ladies, Mrs. Jones lives in Seattle."

My attempt at the social niceties had the effect of creating complete silence. Maybe everyone's hungry, I thought.

"Let me make tea," I said, spooning leaves into the large brown pot I had warmed in the kitchen. I picked up the kettle and poured. "Would anyone like a scone or a piece of shortbread?"

Doris gazed at the plump little terrier. She shifted her eyes to the other two women. "You come out here every year for the dog's birthday?" Her voice was incredulous.

Miss Mason looked at her watch. "Oh, dear, look at the time. We have a dinner reservation in Willow Falls. Perhaps we might have a piece of shortbread for the road?"

Miss Gray quickly stood up. "I had no idea it had gotten so late. I was so enjoying trouncing Georgina at checkers. We'll just let ourselves out the side door near the carts. Is it truly all right to leave dear Rollo here with you?"

"Of course," I said, wrapping a paper napkin around four squares of shortbread. I handed it to Miss

Mason. "He won't be any trouble. Where did you decide to have dinner?"

"We're going to the Bluebird Café," Miss Gray said. "Do you know it?"

"I know it well, and you couldn't have chosen better. Tell them I said hello. And drive carefully. The weatherman says we may get some precipitation in the next day or so."

Miss Mason nodded to Doris and Miss Gray gave her a timid glance as they left the room. Their voices faded as they went down the hall to the side door.

"Aren't they a little young to be talking like that? Geez, they sound like they're about ninety-three," Doris said. "I can't believe they celebrate the dog's birthday. Weird."

Great. Alone with Doris at last.

I lifted the tea pot's lid and peered in, then added a little more water to mix up the brew. "Would you like a cup of tea?" I asked her. Say no, say no, I chanted in my head, say no and go away.

"Sure, I'd love some."

Damn. "So. Doris." Keep going, keep going, I said to myself. "Will your husband be joining us for tea?"

"He said he'd be down in a few minutes. I could really use one of those scones. Are these dogs around all the time?" She looked from Emily Ann to the recumbent Rollo, now snoring as he lay as close to Emily Ann as she allowed; then to Jack, basking in the fire's warmth.

"Yes, the dogs are around all the time," I said firmly. "This inn prides itself on being a haven for dog owners who want to vacation with their pets. Since

114

we're on an island with no cars it's safe for them to be off leash all the time, which some city dogs never get to do. But if you're not comfortable with them I'll be glad to phone around and find another B&B for you."

"Impossible," she said, shaking her head. "I've unpacked."

Great. Just because she was an efficient traveler I was stuck with her. Surreptitiously biting my lip , I poured her tea. "Do you take anything in your tea?"

"Never. Just give it to me straight." She leaned forward in her chair to take the cup and saucer that I carried to her. I set a small plate with a scone on the table at her elbow and returned to the cart to pour my own tea. Then I sat down next to Emily Ann on the settee.

Before she put the cup to her lips, she closed her eyes and breathed in the rising steam. "Mmmm, smells like good tea." She sipped the hot brew and seemed to consider it carefully for a moment. "Is this Darjeeling?"

I gaped like a beached fish. "Well, yes," I admitted.

She was nodding. "Thought so. Good choice."

"You—you know tea!" I could not have been more amazed if she had produced a ukulele from her pocket and started crooning melodies about warm is-land breezes. "Except for Mary Pat, who owns this inn, I never meet anyone who knows tea. Everybody drinks coffee."

She sipped again, then reached for the scone and broke off a piece. "I know," she said. "I live in Seattle, for heaven's sake. Well, you lived there, you know

115

what it's like. I've given up ordering tea in restaurants." She popped the bread into her mouth.

"Oh, me too." This was so weird. Doris and I felt the same way about something. "They bring you a tea bag and water that's not hot enough, and a hunk of lemon, and call it tea. Ig."

"Right. And honey in a little plastic packet. Or if they think they're being fancy you get a whole basket of tea bags, and there's not a decent one among them. This is a good scone, too. Did you bake it?"

I nodded.

"I always wondered what you did with yourself when you were married to Roger. It's for damn sure you weren't hanging out with him in the evenings. Guess you learned to bake."

Ah, the Doris I'd always known. The one who knew just where to stick in the knife and how to twist it. A few months ago this reference to my husband's philandering would have hurt. "I learned to bake from my aunt. It was one of many things Roger didn't appreciate about me," I told her evenly.

There was a moment's silence, then Doris made a face. "There I go again. I keep trying to turn over a new leaf but I've still got the same old mouth."

I had to set my tea cup on the table in front of me. I couldn't believe my ears. Doris—sounding human? Emily Ann stirred and put her head in my lap. I stroked one of her ears while I tried to come up with a reply. "Um..."

She waved one hand at me. "You don't have to say anything. I know what a bitch I can be. I've always been this way. I just blurt stuff out. Then I decided to go to law school and it actually worked for me, so there was never any incentive to stop."

"I—I'm just surprised. I mean, you've always seemed to be completely in control of everything. You're a partner at the law firm, you have clients all over the country. I figured you said the things you did to me because...well, because you saw me as a spineless wimp."

"Well, Roger did walk all over you, but he was such an arrogant bastard that he did that to practically everyone. He left me alone because he never knew what I was going to say to him, or about him for that matter. You should have cut off his dick early on. He would have been a much better husband." She took another bite of her scone and chewed vigorously.

In the setting of the parlor of the Bunny Farm Inn, with the crackling fire and the warm glow from the lamps, her phraseology seemed particularly ludicrous. I started to laugh. She looked at me in surprise, then one corner of her mouth curved up. "Yeah, okay, none of my business."

I shook my head. "No, no—well, of course it *is* none of your business. I was just enjoying the image for a moment. Let's not talk about Roger. I'm still embarrassed that I was married to him for so long. What I want to know is how can you tell you're drinking a particular tea?"

"Blame that one on my grandmother. She went to work in a tea room in Seattle in 1911, when she was twenty years old, and in a couple of years she was running the place. When her father died she inherited a little money and she bought the business and expanded, opened some more tea shops and then became a tea importer. She sold off the shops before World War Two but kept the importing business, though of course importing tea during those years was pretty nonexistent. She branched out into other kinds of importing, but she always loved tea, and she had me drinking it practically out of my baby bottles. One of my earliest memories is of my mother telling her not to give me tea, that it would stunt my growth." She stretched out her long legs and looked at them. "Guess Grandma was right and Mom was wrong."

"And that explains why you're an expert on import law." I got up and took the teapot over to refill her cup, then went back and picked up a scone. It looked pretty plain all by itself. "Hey, I've got some homemade lemon curd. You want some for your scone?"

"Oh, Louisa," she said, shaking her head and grinning. "How wicked you are, and to think I never knew. Sure, bring it on."

"Back in a minute."

She leaned over and picked up the newspaper she had thrown on the floor when she sat down. In the kitchen, just as I touched the handle on the refrigerator, I heard a floorboard creak overhead, then creak again. "What a noisy old house," I said to Jack, who had shadowed me into the room. But Jack went over to the stairs going up from the kitchen, put his feet on the first step, and gazed intently up. He looked back over at me, then back up the stairs.

"Now what?" I hissed at Jack in a whisper. No one should be in the part of the house over the kitchen. That was Mary Pat's suite and the door was locked.

I kicked off my shoes. My wool socks made no noise on the back stairs. I managed to skip the one that chirped, and Jack wasn't heavy enough to trigger its noise. When I reached the upstairs hall, I tiptoed to Mary Pat's door and silently tried the handle. Still locked. I didn't have the key on me. I'd left the whole ring of keys in my jacket pocket, which for once was hung neatly in the coat closet near the front door. It would be quicker to go down the front stairs.

I hurried down the back hall and around the corner into the main hall, and ran straight into Mr. Jones. The collision knocked the air out of me in a small shriek. He grabbed my upper arms to keep me from careening back, then dropped his hands when I was steady on my feet again. Jack came bustling up to stand between us, though his enthusiastically wagging tail detracted from any appearance that he was guarding me.

"I'm sorry," he said. "I got turned around, I guess. I was trying to go downstairs."

"Did you hear anything up here a couple of minutes ago?" I asked him.

He shook his head. "No, I was in my room shaving. Why?"

As far as I could tell, no one but William Jones had been upstairs. I had definitely heard the floorboards creak over the kitchen, but I could think of no reason Doris's husband would have been snooping around.

"I guess it was nothing. Just old house noises," I said. "Let me take you down the back way and we can pick up the lemon curd on the way to the parlor."

"Lead on." He gestured with a graceful hand. "This house is big enough to need a guide. What in the world is lemon curd? It sounds lumpy."

I led him down the back stairs, saying over my shoulder, "If you've never had it, you're in for a treat. At least I think so. Come and try some on a scone and have a cup of tea."

When we reached the parlor, Doris was hidden behind the newspaper. Mr. Jones crossed the room to his wife and leaned over the sheets of paper in her hand to plant a kiss on the top of her head.

"Oh, hi," she said, lowering the paper and smiling up at him.

"Anything good in the paper?" he asked, then went over to the settee where Emily Ann still reclined. "Excuse me, you beautiful thing, may I join you?"

Emily Ann batted her short eyelashes at him and sat up. Her whippy tail beat a welcome on the upholstery. William Jones sat down and looked at her admiringly.

"This is a very handsome dog," he said. "Was she a racer?"

"She was," I acknowledged, "though she wasn't fast enough to do it for long. Emily Ann, lay down," I told her. I poured another cup of tea and put a scone on a plate, and took them over to him. Emily Ann curled up beside him. Together they filled the length of the small sofa. "Would you like to try that lemon curd on your scone?"

"Sure thing. Even if it's not lumpy."

"Lumpy?" Doris asked.

"Your husband never heard of lemon curd and thought it sounded lumpy," I explained, picking up the curd container and a spoon. I let each of them place some on their plates. Then I retrieved my own cup and sat down in the rocking chair. The brew had cooled while I was out of the room but was still drinkably warm.

Mr. Jones broke off a bite of scone and added some lemon curd, then popped it in his mouth. He chewed and swallowed, then said, "I see what you mean. Smooth and rich. Very nice." He ate another piece.

I looked over at Doris. She was being uncharacteristically quiet, and I saw that she was reading again. She must have felt my eyes on her, for she lowered the paper.

"There's an interesting article here," she said, "about counterfeiting in Las Vegas, and since we were just there I got sucked into reading it."

I felt my attention sharpen. "Counterfeiting?" I repeated. "You mean like twenty dollar bills? I would have thought casinos were adept at recognizing fake bills."

"I'm sure they are," she said, "but this article is about counterfeit traveler's checks. It must be part of that series of articles they were running in the Vegas paper." She glanced down at the paper. "Yeah, it's from a syndicate."

I almost dropped my teacup. "You're kidding!"

She stared at me. "Been doing a little creative printing? That doesn't seem like you, Louisa."

"Of course not. But we've had a spate of fake traveler's checks show up around here, including at my cousin's store."

"Really?" Mr. Jones leaned forward to peer at me. "Tell me about it."

"There's not really much to tell. The fakes are really good, and they've been used by several different people—"

"Different people?"

"Both men and women, and varying ages. My cousin has a theory that they're all members of the same family because they're a similar body type."

He nodded, his eyes narrowed as he looked at me. I began to feel a little uncomfortable at his intense interest. An image of what I had found in the office earlier in the afternoon flashed into my brain, and I pushed it away.

"What does the article say?" I turned to Doris to ask.

She stood up. "Here, you can read it. I need to get ready if we're going out to find some dinner." She folded the paper and tossed it to me. "Thanks for the tea, it was just what I needed."

I watched her leave the room. It seemed odd that she had so little to say. I thought back over the years to social events for my husband's law firm, and at all of them you could hear Doris's voice rising over the hum of the crowd. "Is she okay?" I asked her husband, who was stroking Emily Ann's smooth gray head.

He smiled at me. "She's fine. We had to get up early to catch our plane and she was up late gambling. She's just tired."

"Did you say you'd come from Las Vegas? I thought Mary Pat said you had made your reservation from somewhere back east."

"Yes to both," he said. "Getting married in a tacky Vegas wedding parlor appealed to our senses of humor, so that's what we did, but a couple of days there was enough."

"How did you happen to pick this place?"

"Doris found it on the Internet. She said she liked this area when she was here before, that the shopping was great and there are decent restaurants, and this particular inn sounded like a good place to honeymoon."

"Well, it does help if you like dogs," I said. "I'll have to look at Mary Pat's web site again and see if it's clear that there are likely to be dogs here. Doris seemed surprised to see them."

He looked down at Emily Ann. "Well, I love dogs and I don't get to be around them enough. This is a treat for me. Especially now that the little guy has stopped barking."

We looked at Rollo, lying on his back and snoring. He chuffed and whimpered and his feet ran a few steps in the air, and then he went back to snoring. "He does have a lot to say," I agreed. "Even in his sleep. Have you and Doris been planning to marry for a long time? I lost touch with everyone I knew in Seattle when I moved back here, and I didn't know her terribly well anyway."

"No, we only met recently," he said. "I'd better see when she wants to go out. Is there anywhere relatively close for a drink and dinner?"

"There's a rustic steakhouse sort of place at Miller's Crossroads, about eight miles from here." I thought for a moment. "And if you go in the other direction, toward Willow Falls, there's a little town called Radford which has a bar where you can get a beer and some probably pretty bad sandwiches. Of course you should take into account that I don't do bars, and I'm a food snob."

"Still, sounds like our options are limited. Anything else?"

"Well, I'd go into Willow Falls, which is about forty miles. I was just telling Miss Mason and Miss Gray how good the Bluebird Cafe at Third and Maple is. Maria's Cucina is a pretty good Italian place. Or if you like spicy there's the Beau Thai Restaurant."

"They all sound more promising than a beer and a dried out sandwich. I'll check with Doris and see what she'd like to do. Thanks for the tea," he said. He gave Emily Ann one last pat and stood with fluid grace, then headed for the door.

"Don't get lost again," I called after him. "Up the main stairs, and the first door on the right is yours."

"Thanks," he said as he disappeared around the corner. A moment later I heard his firm tread going up the stairs.

I looked around the cozy room at the three sleeping dogs, then picked up the newspaper to read the article that Doris had found.

The phone rang.

I rose and hurried to the office, catching the phone on its fourth ring. "Good evening, Bunny Farm Inn," I said into the receiver.

124

"Hey! Lou! It's me. Sorry I couldn't talk to you earlier." It was Kay's familiar voice.

"That's okay."

"I had some customers in the store and they were the kind who want to know the story behind every object," she went on.

"Did they buy anything?"

"Sure did, they—"

The phone gave the clicking sound that signaled another incoming call. "Kay, hold on," I told her. "I've got another call and it may be someone I have to pick up."

"That's okay, I'll just talk to you tomorrow when Ambrose and I come out for dinner," she said, and hung up. I scowled. I wanted to talk to her. I picked up the other call. "Bunny Farm Inn."

"Yes, this is Bradley Potter. You said to call when I was getting close."

"Oh, yes, Mr. Potter. I'll drive down to the bridge to meet you. How far away are you?"

"I passed Radford a few minutes ago."

"Ah, not far. I'll come right down then. Do you have much luggage? Will you need a cart to get it across the bridge?"

"Yes, that would be very helpful. I have a number of cases."

"All right. I'll see you at the parking area."

Damn, another trip across the floating bridge. I started out of the office. My hand froze, hovering over the light switch. Radford? Hadn't he said he was coming from High Cross? I was sure I'd told him to call from Miller's Crossroad, not Radford. I wondered if he had gotten lost and been wandering around the countryside, then shrugged. I flicked down the light switch and went to find my coat.

13

In the gleam from the light over the parking area, Mr. Potter appeared to be entirely gray. Gray hair, gray calf-length coat open over gray sweater and slacks, gray shoes.

Tubby was the word that came to mind as he climbed out of his gray-white Audi four-door sedan. He was about my height, with a lot of weight carried in his midsection. He approached me with one of those swooping handshakes that car salesmen use. His grip was firm as he pumped my hand up and down, though he had small hands. "Brandon Potter," he announced. The neatly trimmed mustached perched upon his upper lip was also grayed by the light.

"Good evening," I said, retrieving my hand. "I'm Louisa McGuire. Welcome to the Bunny Farm Inn." Hadn't he told me his first name was Barton? Perhaps I had heard it wrong. "Are your bags in the trunk?"

"Sure are. Let me get this thing open." He jingled a set of keys and used one to open the trunk lid. I pulled the cart used to convey baggage across the bridge over to the car. An amazing amount of luggage filled the trunk. Two big suitcases, one mid-sized, a duffle bag, a square, leather-covered vintage overnight case, a couple of canvas bags, and a pink cardboard bakery box. He carefully lifted out the latter, and left the rest of the bags for me to handle. I wondered if he had a bad back. With some effort I pushed the load across the lot and onto the bridge.

By now I had gone across this thing enough times that I was able to hold my bridge phobias at bay. It helped that the water near shore was shallow enough to have frozen, even though there had not been enough cold weather this winter to freeze the whole lake. I didn't truly believe the ice was solid enough to hold me. But at least it wasn't visually heaving up and down, which would make me dizzy and feeling like the bridge was also heaving. The wheels of the heavily laden cart made ker-chunking noises as they ran over each board in the bridge, and the cold wind encouraged me to hurry. Mr. Potter trotted along behind.

When we reached the island he settled into the station wagon with the pink box on his lap. I scowled as I heaved the bags into the back of the car. Did he think this was the Ritz? In spite of the cold, the exertion was enough to make me sweat inside my layers of sweater, coat, mufflers and gloves. He'd better have a bad back or I'd be annoyed at his rude behavior.

When I finished stowing his luggage and pushed the cart back into the garage, I paused for a moment to take a deep breath. It had been a very long day. I had had some unwelcome surprises. Now I had a guest who seemed to be under the impression that my role at the Bunny Farm Inn was that of handmaiden. I was seized with a longing to find Bob and be enfolded in his arms and hear him say, "There, there, everything's okay now." Short of that, hearing Kay snort when I told her about Potter not helping with the cases might be enough.

I exhaled and watched my breath hang in the cold night. Onward to the inn, I told myself, and returned to the driver's seat of the car.

"It's not far to the house," I said by way of small talk, as I started the engine. "It's too bad you couldn't have gotten here earlier in the day. The island is quite lovely. But you'll be able to see it tomorrow. Did you come far today?"

"I did, rather," he said, and that was all.

After a moment I said, "Ah. Well, you'll be able to have a relaxing time while you're here. The room I've given you is away from the other guests who are staying this weekend."

"Good. I think I mentioned that I'm a light sleeper. I thought a bed and breakfast might be a better choice than a hotel this time of year. Quieter, you know."

I thought of Rollo. Quiet was hardly his middle name. This was starting to feel like one of those scenarios I imagined when I first heard of minding an inn. "Um, we'll do our best to see that you aren't disturbed," I told him, mentally crossing my fingers and hoping it would prove true.

We were silent for the rest of the ride to the house. I pulled up under the porte-cochère, as close to the side door as I could get. "Let's get your luggage in, and then I'll register you," I said, hoping he would take the hint that he should help schlep the things. "You can set your box on the table just inside the door."

I used the lever on the floor by my seat to pop open the back of the car, and went back and pulled out the square overnight case and one of the canvas bags, then lead the way up the steps. Mr. Potter followed, carrying his pink box. As I opened the door, I heard the sound of dog feet rapidly approaching, and Rollo barking. I should have shut all three dogs into the kitchen before I left. Too late now. They charged around the corner and surrounded me and Mr. Potter.

"Get away!" he cried, holding the pink box aloft. "Down! You certainly weren't joking about there being dogs."

As soon as Mr. Potter spoke, Rollo began leaping at him. Apparently his nap had had a revivifying effect.

"Rollo, off," I commanded, but it did not seem to be something that Miss Mason and Miss Gray had taught him. I set down my burdens, pushed Emily Ann aside, and managed to snag the leaping terrier. He wiggled to get down but I kept a firm grip.

"I'm sorry, I should have shut them away until you had time to get settled. I do apologize. Let me put them in another room while you bring in your cases."

I tucked Rollo firmly under one arm, and patted my leg with the other hand. "Come on, dogs, let's go get a cookie," I said to them, and hurried toward the kitchen. Emily Ann and Jack followed obediently. Rollo squirmed in my grip until we were in the kitchen. I closed the door firmly and set him down, then went to the cabinet where there was a box of dog biscuits. When I turned back, my two dogs were sitting expectantly two feet away with that eager, attentive look dogs get when food is in the offing. Rollo was at the door, trying to dig his way under it. He snuffled at the crack and then barked.

I gave Jack and Emily Ann each a biscuit. "Rollo, here," I called in an encouraging tone of voice. He ignored me and kept digging. Maybe that wasn't his call word. "Rollo, come!" I tried again, with the same results—none. I went over and waved a piece of biscuit under his nose. It was fragrant enough to catch his attention, and I tossed it a few feet away. When he scrambled over to grab it, I slipped through the door and quickly shut it behind me, then leaned against it to catch my breath. And to give Mr. Potter time to bring in his own damn suitcases. From the other side of the door I heard the sounds of renewed digging and barking. I hoped the flooring was as resilient as the manufacturers no doubt claimed it was; he was a very determined little terrier.

After a while I straightened, squared my shoulders, and returned to where I had left Mr. Potter. I was gratified to see that more of the luggage had been carried in, the duffle and the other canvas bag, and the midsize suitcase. I started out the door to help with what was left and encountered Mr. Potter pulling one of the big cases toward the steps.

"Here, let me hold the door for you," I offered.

He grunted as he heaved the case up the stairs and through the door. I let the screen bang, then went down to the car for the last case. It hadn't gotten any lighter since I had wrestled it in here, but I got the thing out and set it on the drive, then dropped the trunk lid. The suitcase was equipped with wheels, so I rolled it over to the steps, expecting that Mr. Potter would open the door for me. It stayed closed. Several seconds passed. Either I would have to manage by myself, or yell at the tubby guy to open the door.

I was suddenly very sure that if I started to yell at him for anything I would have a very hard time stopping. And if he didn't like being yelled at and wanted to leave I would have to put all his luggage into the car and drive him to the bridge and reload the cases on the cart and push them across the bridge and dump them by his car and run as fast as I could back across the damned floating bridge and jump into the car and career through the night to the Bunny Farm Inn and run inside and lock the door behind me and dash upstairs to my room and scream and scream and scream.

I took a deep breath. I hadn't known I was so close to the edge. Pressing my lips together firmly, I lifted the big suitcase, hefted it up the steps, and managed to open the screen and the door and get the thing inside. Mr. Potter was nowhere to be seen. All his luggage was there, the pink box was still on the table by the door, but there was no tubby little man in sight. I looked around, and saw that the door to the office was ajar. Light streamed out into the hall. I hurried there and found him looking around the room as though he owned it.

"I see you found the office," I said, my tone higher than normal.

"Yes. Is this where we do the formalities?"

"Yes, it is. Please fill out this form and let me have your credit card."

His handwriting was back-slanted, cramped, almost printing. Neither of us spoke until I handed back his card. I noticed that he didn't put it back into his billfold, but just stuck it into his coat pocket. After what Mary Pat had said, I thought I'd better pay attention to these details in case he wanted to sue me later.

In the light of the office, the shades of gray I'd seen in the parking area changed into more normal colors. His hair was medium brown, the square little mustache a shade or two darker. His face was very smooth and pale except for the pink of the plump cheeks, and his eyes were a very dark blue. His coat became camel brown, and the slacks and sweater were both navy. The shoes, however, were still a dark gray.

"Here is your room key, and one for the golf carts." I took his registration form. "In case you want to get to the bridge and back. Breakfast is in the dining room, any time until ten in the morning. If you'd like afternoon tea, we serve it in the small parlor at about four. I can show you where that is. Books and magazines are in the library, and if you'd like to listen to music there is a CD player in there as well."

Footsteps sounded overhead, running down the stairs. In a moment Mr. Jones looked into the office.

"Hi," he said, "here you are. Oh, I'm sorry, I didn't know you were busy."

"Just finishing," I told him. "I'm ready to take Mr. Potter up to his room. Mr. Potter, Mr. Jones and his wife are staying for the weekend as well."

William Jones came into the office, and the two men shook hands. Then he turned to me and said, "I wanted to let you know we're going to take your advice and drive into Willow Falls for dinner. I'm not sure what time we'll be back. Will the door be unlocked?"

"I'll leave the side door open until ten," I told him. "Give me a call if you'll be any later than that and I'll let you in."

I led both of them back out into the hall, where William noticed the pile of baggage. "Let me help you carry this upstairs," he offered.

I could certainly understand what Doris saw in this man.

"Thanks, that would be great," I told him. Mr. Potter didn't say anything; perhaps he considered it his due.

I grabbed the medium suitcase and a canvas bag and led the way upstairs. William picked up both large cases with no apparent effort and followed.

Mr. Potter brought up the rear, carrying his pink box.

When we reached the top of the stairs, I led the two men along the hall, around the corner to the last door on the left. I set down the canvas bag to open the door, reached in and flipped the light switch. Then I stood back to let them enter. The Oak Room was warm and inviting. I had turned the gas fire on low before leaving to pick up Mr. Potter, and my efforts with the flowers had turned out well.

William put the two cases next to the bed. "There you go. We'll see you later." And he was out of the room. I heard him calling, "Dorrie? Honey, are you ready to go?"

I put the suitcase and bag on the bed, then turned to Mr. Potter. "The fireplace is gas and turns on and off with the key at the side, and supplies for making tea are on your table. I've left a couple of extra quilts there on the window seat. Will you be going out for dinner this evening? I can call somewhere for a reservation if you like."

"No, thank you," he said, looking down at the pink box still in his hands. "I took your advice and picked up something on the way out here. I'm just going to take a hot bath and settle in with a book."

"Sounds like a plan," I said, heading for the door. "If you need anything in the next hour or so, I'll be in the parlor or the kitchen. Have a nice night." I pulled his door shut behind me and walked down the hall.

As I turned into the main hall, the door to the Jones's room opened and Doris strode out. "This better be good," she said over her shoulder to William, who followed her into the hall.

"It will be, darling, it will be," he assured her.

Neither of them noticed me, and they ran down the stairs. I followed slowly, giving a sigh of relief when I heard the door close behind them. I descended the last few stairs and looked down the hall past the office door. Mr. Potter's other canvas bag and the little overnight case remained. No doubt a truly fine hostess would take them up to him. I turned the other way and left them sitting there. If he wanted them, he could come and get them.

I went through the living room and dining room to the small parlor and was about to fall down on the sofa when I remembered that the dogs were still in the kitchen. I heard Rollo, digging and barking. I sighed and headed their way, thinking I'd better release him before he ended up in China.

14

I can nearly always fall asleep. I just can't stay asleep. I'm very familiar with three a.m., the ideal time to stare into the darkness and worry. Where is your husband and what is he doing; how can you make people work together productively when they hate each other; what are your camp mates going to do to you while you're asleep; why doesn't your mother like you as much as your aunt does; why didn't you do that geometry homework that's due tomorrow; how messy are all those bathrooms going to be in the morning; did you get everything you needed to make dinner for Kay and Ambrose; how much fun is Bob having in San Francisco; what's going on at the Bunny Farm Inn?

What the hell *was* going on at the Bunny Farm Inn?

I fell asleep a little after ten. All the guests had returned, and I'd locked the doors, banked fires, peeked at the brioche dough rising in the fridge, given

Jack and Emily Ann their last cookie of the day, and retired with them to my room. I got ready for bed, which wasn't so much a matter of undressing as of changing the clothes I wore for public display for ones that would make sleeping in a chilly room comfortable. Once the bed warmed up from my body heat (and the dogs') I pulled off the socks and the topmost sweatshirt.

I really wanted to talk to Kay. As soon as I settled in bed I tried to call her, but all I got was her answering machine. I didn't bother to leave a message. I phoned the Bluebird, but everyone had gone home there. Then I remembered that this was the opening night of the high school play. Kay and Ambrose would not only be in the audience, but they would be hosting a cast party afterwards at Ambrose's house, as they had for the last twenty-seven years.

I hesitated for a moment, then dialed Ambrose's home number. The phone rang, and rang again, and partway through the third ring it was answered. "Hello?" The voice was very young.

"Yes, hello. May I speak to Kay Chelton, please?"

"Oh, sure. Hang on. I'll have to go find her."

"Thank you."

In the background I heard music and laughter. Whoever answered the phone laid down the receiver with a thunk and said to someone, "Have you seen Miss Chelton?"

"I saw her in the kitchen," came another young voice. Presumably the first young voice went off to find Kay. I waited and listened to music I would normally never encounter and voices that waxed and waned as the party goers moved around Ambrose's house. I heard a high pitched shriek, then someone said, "Justin, you dog, stop it! No! Oh, you are so going to pay!" Evidently Justin's payment was to be extracted near the telephone because the next sound was a loud crash in my ear. I assumed the phone had fallen to the floor, a theory that was confirmed when I heard, "There, see, you knocked the phone down." But these were well bred children. They picked up the phone and hung up the receiver. A dial tone buzzed in my ear.

I gave up on Kay and decided I would read until Bob called me, certain that he would. He didn't. The damned phone, which had rung incessantly the night before, might have been disconnected for all the calls I got tonight.

After a period of staring at the same page and taking nothing in, I decided I could try Kay again at home at about 11:30. So of course I nodded off over my book. When I awoke at four minutes past three it was too late; she would think someone had died. I knew from the fact that there was no glue left on my eyelids that I would not go back to sleep any time soon. I sat up and tucked pillows behind me. Jack stirred sleepily, but Emily Ann was used to my being up in the night. Her ladylike snores continued steadily.

I wondered if I should go downstairs and check on Pan, make sure he was still where I'd left him. The part of me that was afraid he would disappear again was equaled by the part of me that didn't want to get out of my warm bed and put my feet on the cold floor. But a moment later I was jolted out of bed by Jack, who came out of a sound sleep into full alert, jumped off the bed and ran to the closed door. He snuffled at it, looked back at me, sniffed once more, looked at me again.

I barely noticed the cold on my feet as I threw back the covers and hurried over to him. He was out in a flash as soon as I turned the knob, heading down the back stairs. I heard Rollo bark from the front of the house, somewhat muffled but sufficiently loud to be audible all over the upstairs. I followed Jack as quickly as I could, not bothering to turn on the stairway lights. Emily Ann hit the floor as I left the room and followed me down, passing me when we reached the kitchen. I followed her to where Jack pawed at the office door.

I threw it open and switched on the light, then stood blinking in the doorway. The dogs ran in and nosed around, but no one was there. After checking out all four corners of the room, Jack came and sat down in front of me.

"They got away?" I asked. "Who was it?" Unfortunately he was mum on that point.

Emily Ann pushed past us into the hall and turned right. I turned on the hall light, then hurried after her. She trotted up the stairs and paused on the landing halfway up the main staircase. I followed her as far as the landing. She smiled up at the assembled guests, who were all standing at the top of the stairs. Mr. Potter was in front, looking down at me with a frown. Next to him were Miss Mason and Miss Gray, who was holding Rollo. The terrier strained toward Mr. Potter, his short tail wagging madly. Behind them were William and Doris. He looked amused, she

140

looked haughty. Collectively they could have been an ad for a sleepwear company, staring down at me in my tatty old sweats and bare feet.

"Mrs. McGuire, what is the meaning of this disturbance?" demanded Mr. Potter.

"Yes, is everything all right? Is someone down there?" Miss Mason wanted to know.

I continued up the stairs toward them, though I would have preferred to retreat instead of advance, and halted four or five steps from the top. "I don't know. Doesn't seem to be anyone around, but Jack heard something. He's very reliable. I'll check the downstairs. You can all go back to bed. I'm sorry you were awakened."

Doris immediately turned to go back to her room. I heard her say, "What makes you think we were asleep?" William reached out and put his hand on the back of her neck and gave her a little shake that looked affectionate and playful. I thought that if anyone else had tried that with Doris, he would be nursing the stump where the hand used to be. Love is an amazing thing.

"Dorrie, behave yourself," he said. "I'll go down and help Louisa check for the boogeyman." He released her, shouldered his way through the other guests, and started down the stairs.

Mr. Potter flounced a little as he turned to go back to his room, and Rollo succeeded in getting loose from Miss Gray. He bounced over to Mr. Potter and started jumping on him. Mr. Potter stood still and glared at the dog. "Please, madam, control this creature," he sniffed.

Miss Mason grabbed at Rollo and missed, then grabbed a second time and managed to capture the bouncing dog. "I'm so sorry," Miss Gray said. "He really seems to like you."

The two women turned away and I let out my breath. I didn't know I was holding it, but all of this activity was taking place at the top of the stairway. I was relieved that they moved away from the spot where they could have a misstep and come tumbling down—on top of me.

I went back down the stairs, William, Emily Ann and Jack following. "Let's split up," I said to William. "Go down the hall past the office, and take a look outside when you pass the side entrance. I'll meet you in the kitchen."

"Sure you don't want me to stick with you?" he asked.

"Well, just in case the boogeyman really is here, I don't want him to be able to dodge us by looping through the rooms ahead of us," I explained.

William nodded. "A tactical maneuver," he said. "Good deployment of your troops, General." He gave me a snappy salute, turned on his bare heel and headed down the hall. Emily Ann followed him, looking up at his face and smiling as she went.

"Come on, Jack," I said to my aide-de-camp. We went into the large parlor, then the dining room, then the small parlor, turning on lights as we went. I led Jack through the butler's pantry into the kitchen, where William awaited. When I raised my eyebrows at him questioningly, he saluted again.

"Nothing to report, General," he said. "The southern corridor is clear."

"Thank you, Private Smith," I played along. "The northern route proved similarly uneventful."

"I did notice it's beginning to snow, though," he added in a more normal voice.

"Really?" I went to the window and peered out. "Not very much though. I bet it won't amount to anything. We've had a very mild winter."

"Jack probably heard a mouse or something. I'll head back up to bed."

"Ah, the boogeymouse," I said. "You have to keep an eye out for him."

He laughed and went up the back stairs. I hoped he remembered the way to his room from there. The last thing I needed was to have him wandering about and disturbing Mr. Potter again.

I turned and looked out the window. A handful of white flakes drifted slowly down. I hoped we'd get enough to cover the ground; it would be fun to play in the snow with the dogs tomorrow. Then I thought, no, later today. "Come on, you dogs," I said to my companions. "Let's see if we can go back to sleep for another hour or two before we have to get up and make breakfast."

Just before I reached the stairs, I remembered my brioche dough. I took it out of the fridge and left it sitting on the counter so the chill would pass off. I would bake it as soon as I came down again to fix breakfast. And then Emily Ann, Jack and I went back to bed.

15

I had imagined that the guests would deploy themselves in shifts for breakfast. The two women would be up early to take Rollo out to play in the snow. The honeymooners would come down late for breakfast if at all. And Mr. Potter would slot himself in between the others and eat in peaceful solitude.

However, none of them seemed to be able to read my mind and follow instructions.

Perhaps it was the smell of baking brioche that they all found irresistible. The sound of water running from overhead alerted me to the imminent arrival of the first breakfasters.

Besides the brioche I put out cranberry muffins, yogurt, granola, a variety of jams in vivid little china dishes, and a platter of sliced cheeses. There was a carafe of strong French-roasted coffee on a warmer, and I plugged in an electric burner to keep a kettle of boiling water at the simmer level for tea. I had two teapots warmed, and there was fresh mint or a Ceylon-Darjeeling blend to brew. The sideboard in the dining room's bay of windows held an assortment of china plates, cups and saucers, mugs, and heavy silverware. The table was laid with a cheerful tablecloth in a forties fruit print, and the cotton napkins picked up the rosy pink in the print. I had enough provisions laid out for two or three people, and more in the kitchen to bring out as needed.

I heard footsteps coming down the front stairs and a then woman's voice, and I stepped into the dining room to welcome Miss Mason and Miss Gray to breakfast. It proved instead to be Mr. and Mrs. Jones, he with an arm thrown casually around her shoulders.

"Something smells great," William said, smiling at me. "Sorties in the night always make me extra hungry."

"Well, that's a new name for it," said Doris. I kept a bright uncomprehending expression on my face. "By the way, how is your Mr. Robertson?" she asked me.

"It's Richardson, and Bob is fine, thank you. Help yourselves to breakfast. I'll bring more hot water in a few minutes to keep your tea going."

Before either of them could reply, Miss Mason and Miss Gray arrived, laughing about something. "Oh, hello," said Miss Mason. "Have you had breakfast already?"

"We just got here," William said.

"Well, you're in for a treat." Miss Mason replied. "Mrs. McGuire puts out a wonderful spread."

"Thanks," I said. "Help yourselves, everyone." I retreated to the kitchen. Even though I am very much a morning person, I don't like to talk to anyone early in the day. I just want to go quietly about my business.

Emily Ann had stayed upstairs, snuggled into the blankets on the bed, but Jack was in the kitchen, lying on the rug in front of the Welsh dresser with his head on his paws. He thumped his tail when he saw me. "Breakfast has begun," I told him. "We'll check later when they're all done to see if they dropped anything. I'll let you do the floors."

I puttered around for five or six minutes, putting dishes in the dishwasher and wiping countertops. Then I donned what I hoped was a pleasant expression and went back to the dining room to see if all was well. Mr. Potter had just arrived and was pouring himself a cup of coffee.

"Ah, Mrs. McGuire," he said, noticing me. "I'd like my eggs poached, if I may."

An image of my husband swam before my eyes. He used to demand poached eggs in the same tone of voice. Roger even used to call me Mrs. McGuire in a smug, proprietary way, loving both the sound of his own name and the chance to remind me of my place. I took a deep breath to control my voice. "I'm sorry, Mr. Potter, we do a continental breakfast here. Is there enough cereal and yogurt on the buffet? Let me go get some more bread."

I turned on my heel and retreated through the butler's pantry to the kitchen, where I stood leaning on the door for a moment. Calm down, Louisa, I told myself. The man didn't know you don't do a hot breakfast. Wherever it was he heard about the inn, or read about it, he must have missed the description of the breakfast.

I squared my shoulders and went over to the counter, where another basket of bread was ready to take out. I grabbed it and a bowl of soft butter and headed back for the dining room. Since my hands were full, I leaned sideways to push open the swinging door into the dining room, and I heard Doris's voice. I paused to listen before making an appearance.

"—cantaloupes you find in the store don't begin to scratch the surface of what is possible in melons," she was saying. Oh, good, I thought, they're talking about fruit. Not much room for discord there. "Of course, since they originally come from China—"

"I thought they originated in the Middle East," Mr. Potter put in.

I opened the door a little further and peeked through. Doris glared at Mr. Potter, her mouth tight. She is not accustomed to being corrected. Few people would dare. William slid neatly into the little silence. "We'll have to look that up," he said. "Perhaps there's an encyclopedia somewhere, or maybe we could borrow the computer in the office and check online."

I pushed on into the room and crossed to the buffet. "More brioche and muffins," I announced. I grabbed the depleted bread basket, then hefted the tea kettle and noted that it was getting light. "I'll bring some more boiling water in a moment so you can refresh your tea."

"Thank you," Miss Gray said politely as I headed back for the kitchen. I gave a little acknowledging wave with the basket before I went through the door.

I turned up the heat under the kettle I had warming on the stove. When steam came out of the spout I flicked off the gas and picked up the kettle. Back to the butler's pantry, and a short pause for listening at the door to the dining room. This time it was Miss Mason's voice I heard.

"—true that twins are becoming much more prevalent, and even triplets and other multiple births are increasing. The school where I teach is small, less than two hundred children, and we currently have seven sets of twins attending."

"Good grief. One child would be trouble enough without having a litter," Doris said as I entered the room.

Miss Gray replied mildly, "It certainly is more effort to raise twins, but their families seem to love them."

I went again to the buffet, casting an eye at their plates as I passed the table. Everyone was eating still. The granola was running low, but everything else seemed to be plentiful.

"Would anyone like more granola?" I asked the assembled breakfasters.

"I've had plenty," Doris replied, and there were murmurs of agreement.

I picked up the granola bowl and the kettle I was taking back to the kitchen. "How is everything else holding out?" I asked. "Anyone need anything?"

Amid murmurs of "Everything's fine," Mr. Potter said, "I believe the sugar bowl is getting low."

"Ah. Let me refill it," I said. I didn't want to make another trip, so I set the bowl holding the crumbs of granola on the table, put the sugar bowl into it, and then picked up both. Back into the butler's pantry and thence into the kitchen.

"It's a good thing I wear comfortable shoes," I commented to Jack. "Now I know why Cleta wears those trainers. You spend all your time running back and forth in this kind of job." He gave a little woof in response. "Yeah, I know you like to be barefoot. And you like running after people more than I do. Why don't you take the sugar bowl in to Mr. Potter and I'll lay down for a nap?" He panted happily at me.

I set the kettle on the stove and the granola bowl in the sink. I turned the hot water handle on before I remembered that the sugar bowl was there too. "Damn," I muttered, then turned to the Welsh dresser to find another bowl. I took a moment to glare at the Pan figurine. "Excuse me, Jack. I need to get in here." A variety of china objects sat on the lower shelves behind the doors. Jack obligingly got up, stretched, and moved over so I could open the cabinet door. I reached in and pulled out a sugar bowl. This one was cottage ware, shaped like a little house with a lid representing the thatched roof. I straightened, said thanks to Jack, and went back to the counter to give the thing a swipe with my dish towel before scooping sugar into it. Replacing the lid, I carried it toward the dining room. This time it was William's voice I heard as I pushed open the door.

"—most people think so, but it's really the Secret Service that investigates cases of counterfeiting," he was saying in his deep rumble.

I stumbled and dropped the sugar bowl. Fortunately it was not one of the more delicate examples of its kind, and it merely bounced on the carpet. The lid came off and sugar spilled out onto the floor. "Oops," I muttered, and knelt to wipe up as much as I could. If I left the sugar there and went for the vacuum, it would probably get stepped in and tracked around the house. Most likely by me. I imagined a vast army of ants happily trooping through the house, glad to be out of the snow and eating sugar. Now I'd have to go back to the kitchen for yet another sugar bowl. Why couldn't Mr. Potter take his tea straight like Doris did?

I pushed sugar back into the bowl with my fingers, then started to rise. When I looked up, five pairs of eyes were staring at me. I stayed where I was. Getting up from the floor is not my most graceful act, and I could have done with less of an audience.

"Don't mind me," I told them. "I'm going to take this back to the kitchen and get another sugar bowl. Go on with what you were saying, William."

"Oh, we were just talking about that article Dorrie read about counterfeit traveler's checks," he said. "I was mentioning that the Secret Service investigates counterfeiting, not the FBI."

"Ah," I said. They were all still looking. My knees were starting to ache; I couldn't stay down here forever. I feigned pushing a few more grains of sugar into the bowl.

"I thought the Secret Service just protected the President," Miss Gray said, and mercifully that brought their eyes back to each other, all except Mr. Potter who continued to watch me.

"Nope, the Secret Service is part of the Treasury Department," William said knowledgably. He must have been a whiz in his high school civics class. "Which no doubt is how they ended up with counterfeiting."

"And after all, we wouldn't want the President to get stuck with any bogus traveler's checks," Doris said dryly.

"But maybe he could use them to pay off spies or something," Mr. Potter said, finally turning back to the others. "We could buy secrets from other countries without adding to the national debt."

This was more whimsical than I would have expected from Mr. Potter. I took advantage of the moment to push off the floor with one hand and rise to my feet.

"Now, there's a plan," William said to Mr. Potter.

Everyone started talking at once. I fled back to the kitchen. When I went to the Welsh dresser for yet another sugar bowl, I looked at the top shelf and glared at Pan leering down at me over his flute from between the teapots. "Think you're smart, don't you," I growled at him.

A clean, filled sugar bowl in my hands, I returned once more to the dining room. Miss Gray's voice reached my ears.

"—hardly ever get the chance to play in the snow like this. Rollo just loves it. He tries to play with the flakes as they're coming down."

"We had a dog that did that when I was a kid," William said. "Most of the time he slept, but when it snowed he turned back into a puppy."

I went to the unoccupied end of the table, opposite Mr. Potter, and placed the sugar bowl on the table. Again, I found everyone looking at me.

"How is breakfast?" I said.

"Delicious," said Miss Gray, and "I'm stuffed," from William. The others nodded. Miss Gray went on, "We were just talking about how to spend the day. Georgina and I are going to take Rollo into the woods again this morning, and then probably go to High Cross for lunch."

"And Dorrie and I plan to head into Willow Falls about lunch time, do some shopping, and then have an early dinner there as well," William added.

There was a silence which everyone seemed to expect Mr. Potter to fill with his plans. He did not. William finally said, "How about you, Potter? Snow or shopping?"

Mr. Potter gave a parsimonious smile. "Neither, I'm afraid. I have to prepare for a presentation I'm giving on Tuesday. I'll be working through the weekend in my room. I'll run out for some food later in the day, since Mrs. McGuire seems unwilling to provide any meals but breakfast." He pushed back his chair and rose to his feet. "In fact, I'd better get started." He left the room, and his footsteps could be heard going up the stairs a moment later.

Great, I thought. I'll never be able to make his bed or pretend to clean his bathroom. He's bound to be out at the same time I'm gone with Earlene. I looked out the window.

"Well, I hope you've all eaten a big breakfast," I told the others. "You'll need plenty of fuel if you're going out. Looks like it's starting to snow harder."

Everyone turned to look out the windows. "It's so beautiful," Miss Gray breathed. "Rollo will just love this. We'll have to go up and let him out of his crate in a few minutes. Mrs. McGuire, would your dogs like to go out and play in the snow with us?"

"Jack would love it. He never seems to feel the cold," I told her. "Emily Ann would probably think I was insane to suggest such a thing. She declined even to get up this morning."

"There's certainly nothing on her to keep her warm," Miss Mason said. "She's about the sleekest thing I've ever seen. But we'd love it if Jack wanted to come out and play."

"That would be great," I told her. "I have an appointment a little later this morning, so if you get tired of him just put him in the kitchen door. Oh, and make sure the larger dog door in the mud room is locked so he can't go back out."

"Rollo will love to have a playmate," Miss Gray said, and rose from her chair. "I'm going up to our room to start bundling up. Tell Jack we'll be along for him in a few minutes."

Miss Mason got out of her chair as well and the two left the dining room. "I think I'll toddle along as well," William said. "That tub in our bathroom is enormous, and I'm looking forward to having a long luxurious soak in it. Dorrie, I hope we packed my rubber duckies." He dropped a kiss on top of her head as he passed behind her chair, and she turned and caught his hand.

"Well, darling, I don't know about the rubber duckies, but I bet dear little Rollo is not the only one who would like to have a playmate," she said. He laughed and pulled her to her feet, and they left the dining room arm in arm without a backward glance.

16

The scene outside the inn would have had Currier and Ives itching to get to their paintbrushes. Snow had continued to fall through the night, and was now coming down by the basketful. Since there was no wind, the big flakes drifted down at a peaceful pace and piled softly on top of each other. I thought I could hear them land with a sigh.

The porte-cochère sheltered the little station wagon, so it took only a moment to brush the windshield clear. The engine caught when I turned the key, and I drove into the whiteness.

The pine trees along the drive protected it, and the snow was not as deep there. I steered carefully, enjoying the bite of the snow tires grabbing traction. When I pulled up by the floating bridge, I saw Earlene's SUV crunch into the parking lot on the other side. Getting out of the car, I waved to her, and started across the bridge. As soon as I stepped on it my foot slipped, and I grabbed the rail. I hoped my boots had enough traction to get me across. Though if they didn't and I fell, I was well padded with layers of sweaters, jacket, muffler and gloves. I should be safe as long as I didn't roll off into the lake. I took a deep breath and started on, letting it out when I reached to far side.

Earlene drove the car around so that the passenger door was near me. When I opened it and climbed in, she said, "Are you still up for this, Louisa? It's pretty darned snowy."

"Gosh, Earlene, I'd hate for you to have driven out here for nothing," I told her. "What do you think? Are the roads too bad? Do you want to get back home?"

"This buggy can handle anything," she said proudly, and probably truthfully. I had an image of her at a demolition derby, driving her huge vehicle over the wrecked chassis of competing cars. "And it isn't very far over there. A mile or two. It's so close I think maybe it's a sign that this is going to be your house."

I did not share her premonition of fruitful house hunting, but I was willing to go along for the ride. After all, we'd seen every other building for sale in Willow County. We certainly wouldn't want to miss this one.

Earlene followed her own tracks down the lane to the main road, skillfully correcting her vehicle's progress when it began to slide.

"How do you like working at that inn?" she asked. A big pile of snow slid off an overhead branch and obscured the windshield for a moment, but it was light enough for the wipers to clear it off. "Are there really customers this time of year?"

"As a matter of fact, there are," I told her. "More than I expected. Two ladies from High Cross are here with their dog for the dog's birthday, and a couple that just got married in Las Vegas and wanted a quiet honeymoon. And a man who called yesterday. He said he has work to do and needs quiet as well."

We reached the county road and found it covered with snow, but there were tire tracks of other vehicles that must have recently passed. We turned left and drove a little faster than in the lane, though nowhere near Earlene's usual rocketing speed.

"I'm kind of surprised," she said. "Doesn't seem like you'd have that many in such an out-of-the-way place, especially in this weather, but then I guess no one knew the snow was coming."

"True," I agreed, "and no one knew that my housekeeping help was going to get the measles, either."

"The measles! Are you hiring child labor out there?"

"I think Terry's in high school, but we haven't met. The measles came along first."

I gasped a little as the SUV did an interesting fishtail maneuver on a short overpass over a creek. But Earlene had it under control before I'd finished reacting.

"I'm not thrilled about the measles," I admitted. "I don't mind making breakfast, but cleaning bathrooms is not my idea of fun. But it's no big deal for a few days." I spared her my horrible camp memories.

An old red pickup truck passed us going the other way. Earlene and the driver waved at each other. A moment later she put on her right turn signal, and made a slow turn at a rusty mailbox sitting on a post leaning perilously toward the road. I suspected that even without the snow I wouldn't have seen the drive.

"Hmmm, it's deeper here," she said. "Hope this doesn't get too exciting."

I kept still so she could concentrate on driving. The drive was a couple of feet lower than the surrounding fields, and fence posts lined its length. We curved first to the left, then right, then went straight uphill for perhaps two hundred feet. We pulled up in front of a house with snow mounded around the For Sale sign stuck in the yard.

Earlene turned off the engine of her SUV and we sat in silence, looking at the house. The snow still fell heavily, big, fat white flakes that sifted down and settled on top of the already deep pile on the ground. The curtain of white turned the winter woods into a Japanese ink painting. Nothing moved except a single cardinal, his red plumage a brilliant dot of color as he flitted from bush to bush.

"I give up," Earlene sighed. "I just absolutely give up. All I can say to you, Louisa, is that they lied to me. I should have checked out this place before dragging you over here, but I was definitely led to believe that it was a house fit for a human being to live in."

I looked at her in alarm. Her usually square shoulders slumped in defeat. She shook her head slowly, and her mouth was tight. I thought she might be blinking back tears.

"Earlene, maybe it's not that bad inside. You should see Ambrose's lake cabin. From the outside you'd swear it would fall down if you so much as looked at it, then you go in and it's gorgeous."

"Louisa, honey, I appreciate that, but do you honestly believe that we're going to go into that— that—that breeding ground for witches and mice, and see anything gorgeous?" She was still shaking her head. "I must have been nuts to drag you here in all this snow, slipping and sliding, taking you away from your guests at that inn, out in the cold on nothing but a wild goose chase."

I knew she was right. The Addams family would love this house. Not a lick of paint graced its exterior, and the roofline sagged just a little in the center. A too-narrow porch stretched across the front, and the screen door had a relaxed attitude in relation to its hinges. I wondered if summer foliage would improve things, or if the snow was covering raggedy grass, half dead perennials, and rusty old pieces of junk left by former occupants. The house looked as though it had been empty for a long time, and for good reason.

"Well, we've come this far," I sighed. "Let's at least poke our heads inside. We might as well add it to our collection."

The steadily falling snow now reached almost to my knees. I was thankful for my many layers of clothing. Besides, I knew from experience that indoors would be at least as cold. We waded up to the porch, and Earlene pulled an old fashioned skeleton key out of her pocket.

"Wow, you don't see keys like that anymore," I said. "No lock box on this front door?"

"Evidently not," Earlene said. "This is the key the owner gave the listing agent." She inserted it in the lock, gave a quarter turn to the right, and the front door opened. "Not very secure. I hope no tramps are living here."

"How would they even find the place?"

"Oh, word gets around. This house has been empty for some time, and people notice. But for sure no one has walked around the yard in the last little while." She looked around at the pristine covering of snow. Our two sets of footprints were the only disturbance.

We stamped as much snow off our feet as we could, then stepped inside. I had been right about the interior chill level. The windows had no coverings, but the heavy snow filtered the light into something dim and mysterious. The place was absolutely still. We stood in a narrow entrance hall, with a steep set of stairs directly in front of us. French doors closed off the rooms on both sides.

I opened the pair of doors on the left and walked into the dining room. The woodwork had been painted dark green to go with flocked wallpaper. I thought the built-in china cabinet along one wall was probably oak underneath the paint and vinyl that lined the shelves. I walked to the kitchen, or what I supposed was the kitchen because there was a single sink in there. Otherwise the room was bare, and in one corner pieces of the ceiling lay on the floor. Perhaps the roof leaked, or someone could have let a tub overflow. I expected Earlene to make some remark, but she said nothing. Neither of us wanted to disturb the thick silence of the house.

Another door led to a tiny mud room that looked out into a yard made lumpy by snow covering whatever was out there—bushes and maybe a glider. No other houses were in sight. I walked back to the entry and into the bare living room, noting the enormous fireplace on an interior wall, its size out of proportion for the modesty of the house. Again the woodwork had been painted, and the wallpaper was a metallic stripe, coming unglued in places, I shook my head.

"This house is like the Sleeping Beauty, waiting for someone to kiss her and wake her up." I didn't exactly whisper, but my voice didn't want to come out very loud. "Of course it would have to be a prince who saves her, because he'd need a boatload of money and a lot of time on his hands to do it."

"I know," she said. "If anyone had taken care of it, this could be a very nice house. Decent size, big piece of property near the lake. But they redecorated in the sixties and then left it that way, and now it's been abandoned for years. Do you want to bother seeing upstairs?"

"Oh, what the heck," I said. "I'm curious about this huge fireplace. I wonder if there's another like it in one of the bedrooms."

Our footsteps thundered as we tramped up the stairs. Four closed doors faced the small central hall. The front room would be over the living room, so I opened that door and stepped inside. There was indeed a fireplace, but it was much smaller than the one downstairs. Shelves with glass fronted doors were built in on each side. Something small on one of the

162

right-hand shelves caught my eye. It was an Indian-head penny.

"Look, an old penny, Earlene," I said, pulling the door. It was stuck. I tugged again. An antique penny was the least reward we deserved for braving the elements to get here.

Earlene said, "I wonder if it's locked."

I tugged harder, and this time the door flew open. Only it wasn't just the door. The entire shallow cupboard swung out, revealing a space behind it, big enough for two or three people to stand in. We gawped in amazement.

"Well, I swan to goodness," Earlene breathed. "Who would ever have guessed that was back there?"

We beamed at each other. "Did you ever in your life think you would find a real live hidden room?" I said. "Wow. I spent one whole summer of my life hiding in a tree reading books where things like this happened. This is great!"

"More of a hidey hole than a room, but still. I wonder why it's here?" She stepped into the space and made a slow, inspecting turn.

"Mmm, pretty isolated out here. Even more so when the house was built. Maybe they wanted a place where they could feel safe. Hey, is the place old enough to have been here during the Civil War? I wonder if it could have anything to do with the Underground Railroad," I said.

I pulled the door open as far as I could and leaned in for a better look. Brick on the chimney wall, plaster on the others, tall because it went up to the ceiling. Being closed off it had kept it reasonably clean, though dust gets in anywhere and cobwebs festooned the ceiling. I reached in and tapped at the walls, hoping for another secret panel that would lead who knows where, but everything sounded solid. Given the size of the house, any further passages would have to enter another dimension to go anywhere.

"We still haven't found my house," I said, backing out. "But this certainly has made my day." I pushed the door shut on the space.

"This is about the coolest thing that ever happened to me" Earlene agreed. "I expect Nancy Drew to walk through the door any moment."

"I wonder if the owners know?" I said as we headed back down the stairs. "There wasn't anything about it on the listing information, was there?"

"Not a thing, and I'd sure play it up if it were in my own home I was trying to sell. You know what, Louisa..." Her voice trailed off.

I pulled open the front door. The snow was falling harder, and our footprints from the SUV to the porch were nearly obliterated. "Wow, Earlene, it's really coming down."

"Let me lock up this house and get us back to the Bunny Farm," she said. "We don't want to get stuck here."

We tramped to the car. Earlene was so short that the snow was now well above her knees. She opened the vehicle and reached behind her seat, pulled out a broom, and knocked snow off the windows. "There. Now at least we can see when we're headed for the ditch." She climbed in, started the engine and managed a three corner turn in front of the house. We headed down the drive for the road.

"What were you starting to say earlier?" I asked.

"When?" she asked, keeping her eyes forward. We went down the hill at an unusual angle, but she pulled the car straight and put it through the bends at a crawl.

"Just as we were leaving the house. We were talking about whether the owners knew."

"Oh, right. I was just going to ask if you'd wait to mention what we found until I've talked to them. If they don't know, they ought to be told first. And I know a couple of people in the historical society too. They might know if this has any historical importance."

The county road was deserted. As we turned toward the inn, I said, "Sure, no problem. I would have told Kay but it can wait. I can't promise not to think about it though. And of course we may find out that everyone in the county already knows about it but us."

"That would be just our luck, wouldn't it? And of course I'm just dying to tell my sister Gina. She's always lorded it over me because she lives in a house where a President's wife once played cards, but I don't think that holds a candle to finding a real live secret room." She risked a glance over at me and we grinned at each other again. There's nothing like a secret to cement a friendship.

We saw no other cars before we reached the Bunny Farm's drive. Snow completely obscured the sign announcing the inn, and we could barely see the tracks we'd made earlier. But we reached the parking area safely, where I was surprised to see Ambrose's car next to the others belonging to the inn's guests. His was only lightly covered with snow, and the warmth of the engine still melted the flakes that fell on the hood.

"Good heavens," I said, "Kay and Ambrose must be here already. I didn't expect them this early. In fact I really didn't think they would come in this weather."

"Some of us don't take snow very seriously," Earlene opined. "We don't get enough to respect what it can do. Louisa, would you mind if I came in and used your bathroom?" Earlene said.

"Of course not," I said. "Come on."

She unfastened her seat belt and opened her door. "It's the curse of middle aged womanhood," she said.

My "Amen to that" was punctuated by the slam of both car doors. "Don't you want to lock up?" I asked as she turned away from her door.

She shook her head. "I'll only be a few minutes. I don't think anyone other than snowshoe bunnies will be out today."

We crunched our way across the bridge to the inn's car on the other side. Ambrose and Kay had walked to the house; their trail in the snow was still obvious. I knew those golf carts would be useless in a storm.

I used my arm to clear snow off the car's windows, and we climbed in. The wheels spun when I tried to back up. I eased off the gas and tried again very gently, then we were on our way. I was glad of the trees that lined the drive; those and Kay and

166

Ambrose's tracks were my only clues where to steer. I went so slowly it felt like driving in a dream.

At last I pulled under the porte-cochère. "Come on in," I said. "You're in luck, there's a bathroom right inside this door."

"That's good. Although I was kind of hoping to see some of the house. I grew up hearing about it."

"Well, this will make a change," I told her, holding open the screen door. "I can show you a house instead of the other way around."

17

I directed Earlene to the powder room, then headed into the kitchen to take off my wraps. Kay and Ambrose sat at the table with a pot of tea and a plate of cookies between them.

"Hey," I greeted them. "You got away early. Was the drive horrible?" I laid my gloves on the table and unwound the muffler around my neck.

"Hey yourself," said Kay, waving a cookie. "There wasn't a customer within fifty miles of the store so we decided to come on out. I tried to call you but you didn't answer here or on your cell phone."

Oh, pooh, I thought, I forgot the damned thing again. In fact, I couldn't think when I had last seen it. Aloud I said, "I didn't want to take a chance of dropping it in the snow." I slid off my jacket. Ambrose rose and took it from me. "Just hang it over a chair," I told him. "I usually do. Thanks."

"You are most welcome," he said. The jacket was deposited on the chair by the back door, and he returned to the table. "I was almost as surprised that you had gone out as I was by our making it here. This is serious snow."

I turned to Kay. "I've been dying to talk to you. It seems likes months—"

The kitchen door opened and Earlene came in. She smiled at Kay and Ambrose. "Well, good morning," she said. "I see you braved the snow too. I've been showing Louisa a house near here and unfortunately it was just a disaster."

I could see Kay about to make a remark about all the other disasters Earlene had shown me, so I said quickly, "If I wanted to get into renovation, this would be a great one to start on. But I'd rather be able to just live in a place. Earlene, you said you wanted to see this house. Would you like a guided tour or do you just want to wander?"

"Well, if you don't mind I would just love to roam around for a bit. My grandmother was friends with Ms. Haskell's mother, and she used to tell me about this place. She had a pair of mittens made of yarn from the hair of those rabbits they raised, and it was a special treat when she would take them out and let me wear them for a little while."

"Just make yourself at home," I told her. "There's only one bedroom upstairs not occupied, and its door should be open, but the downstairs is kind of fun. Mary Pat has collected a lot of stuff."

"I'll just pretend I'm in a museum and wander around quietly," Earlene said, and gave a little wave as she went back out the kitchen door.

I looked at the clock. It was a couple of minutes past eleven. "I don't suppose you all know if any of the guests are out of their rooms? I need to get the housekeeping done."

"I think the women with the dog are still out," Kay said. "I heard barking in the distance when we were walking in from the bridge."

"Wading in," Ambrose added.

"Oh good. I can at least get their bed made. Can you guys entertain yourselves while I run upstairs?"

"Sure," said Kay, "but how about if I give you a hand? You don't want to be picking up after people all day."

I was about to say I didn't want to be picking up after people at all. But Ambrose had been the one to suggest I come to the Bunny Farm. So instead I said, "Let me see what needs to be done and I'll holler if I need you. Oh, I know, could you start chopping onions for tomato sauce? I was going to have the lasagna made before you got here but there hasn't been time. The onions are in that basket on the counter."

"Sure," she said, and pushed back her chair.

As I headed out of the kitchen I heard a murmur of voices. I checked the dining room, then the small parlor. William and Doris were there. Emily Ann was with them, settled beside William with her head on his lap. She thumped her tail when she saw me.

"Hi," said William. "I was just trying to convince Dorrie that we should go get some lunch. She doesn't trust my snow-driving skills."

"Have you had a lot of experience with it?" I asked.

"Grew up in Minnesota," he said, "so if you count tobogganing I've been driving on snow since I was in kindergarten."

"When you do decide to go out, let me know and I'll drive you to the bridge. Would this be an okay time for me to take care of your room?" I asked them. They both nodded.

"Sure," William said, "that would be great."

I went back to the kitchen to grab my bucket of bathroom supplies. Ambrose and Kay were both working. He had rolled up his sleeves and was sautéing garlic in a big iron skillet, and she was chopping onions on the board that pulled out from under the counter.

"Wow, smells good," I told them.

There was the sound of a door slamming, and excited voices, and barking. My trained ear detected both Rollo's and Jack's voices, with a counterpoint by Miss Mason and Miss Gray.

"Now what?" I said. I dropped the bucket on the back stairs and hurried out of the kitchen. Ambrose turned off the stove, and he and Kay followed.

The noise came from the foyer. Earlene clattered down the stairway; William and Doris and Emily Ann arrived via the living room at the same time. Kay's jaw dropped when she saw Doris. Miss Mason and Miss Gray stood just inside the door, clutching each other and gasping for breath. Rollo barked first at William, then at me, then Doris, and back to William. Then he noticed Earlene and barked at her. Jack hurried over to lean on me, his thick, strong tail whacking the wall.

"What's the matter?" I managed over Rollo's noise. "Are you okay?"

171

"Yes, yes, we're all right," Miss Gray said. "But when I think of what could have happened..."

She had her arm around her taller companion, and I noticed then that Miss Mason's left boot and pants leg were sopping wet from the knee down. Snow had crusted over the wetness, but she was dripping on the wide floorboards of the hall. Kay reached down and picked up Rollo and commanded him to hush, which miraculously he did. I could hear Georgina Mason's teeth chattering.

"It—it was the bridge," she managed to say. "I stepped onto and it went crashing into the lake."

"She needs to get into dry clothes," Miss Gray said. "She has incredible reflexes, or she would have been completely in the water. Let her get dry, and then we'll tell you."

They made their way through the crowd and up the stairs. Ambrose said, "I'll get something to mop up the floor," and disappeared back the way we had come. Earlene came the rest of the way down the stairs just as Doris got a good look at my cousin, who was still holding Rollo.

"You're the woman who works in that antique store in Willow Falls," she said, looking Kay up and down. At their last encounter Kay had refused to sell Doris anything from her store. Doris must not remember meeting Kay at my husband's funeral, but I knew that Kay had not forgotten the things that Doris had said to me that day.

"This is my cousin, Kay Chelton," I said, "who owns OKay Antiques. Kay, I think you've met Doris before, and this is her husband, William Jones."

"Nice to meet you," William said, sticking out his hand toward Kay, who took it with an expression I might interpret as ironic. Before she could say anything I went on.

"And this is Earlene Hofenstadter, my friend and real estate agent." Earlene looked gratified, either by my description or by the warm handshake she received from William.

"How odd to see you so far from Seattle yet again," Kay said to Doris, who opened her mouth to reply but was forestalled by Jack.

He had been hovering near me, but now he charged down the hall to the office door. He pawed and snuffled at the bottom of the door, his wagging tail announcing "Someone is here."

I hurried after him. Since Mr. Potter was the only one missing from our gathering, I thought he must be in there. As I opened the door I searched for a way to politely convey that the office was off limits. I was completely flummoxed by the sight of a teenage boy working at the computer.

"Who the hell are you?" I gasped.

He jumped and turned, and I saw that his face and hands were covered with red spots.

"Um, um, like, I'm Terry?" he said. "I work for Ms. Haskell?"

"But you have the measles," I said. Even if he hadn't called and told me yesterday, it was obvious he was unwell, and the spots were a dead giveaway. "Why aren't you home in bed?"

"I have this big project due at school on Wednesday? And like, I did most of it on this

173

computer? She let me," he hastened to assure me. "But I was like, you know, afraid I wouldn't finish it on time and it's for Mr. Pearlman and he's like, no excuses for anything?"

"Good god, is he still teaching social studies? I had him thirty-seven years ago. He must be ancient. Does he still talk and talk and talk?"

Terry grinned, though his eyes were glittering with fever. "He sure does."

Ambrose had entered the room behind me. He held a bath towel in his hand, I assumed for drying the floors that Miss Mason had dripped on. "Terry Jenkins," he said. "You're supposed to have the measles. How did you get here? Does your mother know you're out?"

Terry looked abashed. "Oh, hi, Ambrose," he said, proving once again Kay's contention that Ambrose knows everyone. "No, she's like, at work? And my grandma is coming over to stay with me? Only she called to say she couldn't, like drive in the snow? And like, well, I didn't tell her that my mom had already left. I'm old enough to stay by myself. And I rode over here on my scooter? I figured I could grab my computer files and get back home before anyone knew I was gone?"

Ambrose was shaking his head. "You rode that Vespa in this snow? You are insane, young man. One of us will drive you back home in a few minutes. Someone who's already had the measles. And I'll be calling your mom. You shouldn't be alone when you're sick. Measles can be serious."

Argumentative voices sounded from the foyer, growing louder. Kay and Doris. I needed to separate them before they reached the hair-pulling stage of their conversation.

"Terry, this was a crazy thing to do. Finish downloading your file, and we'll get you home," I said, trying to sound stern. "Ambrose, we need to go rescue Kay. Or Doris. Or both of them."

We left Terry at the computer and headed for the entry. William and Earlene had drifted a few feet into the living room and were talking. But Kay and Doris were right where I had left them, identical glares on their faces. Kay still held Rollo, who for once was not barking, but swiveled his head back and forth between them as though at a verbal tennis match.

"—ashamed to browbeat a woman who never did you any harm—" my cousin growled.

"—arcane business practices that amount to—" spat Doris at the same time.

Ambrose stepped between them and waved the cloth he still held. "Ladies, will you excuse me? I want to get this water wiped up before it marks the floor."

They took a step apart, and Ambrose knelt on the floor and swabbed at the puddle shining on the oak boards.

"Kay, would you put the tea kettle on?" I asked her. "I want to get something hot into Miss Mason."

Kay looked like she still had plenty to say to Doris, but contented herself with, "Sure, Louisa." She set Rollo down and followed her chin toward the kitchen. The kitchen door closed more loudly than usual, but wasn't quite a slam. Rollo barked at the noise, then at

175

me, then ran a few steps into the living room and barked at William and Earlene.

Footsteps sounded on the stairs. I looked up, expecting Miss Gray, but saw Mr. Potter.

"Is all this noise really necessary?" he snapped, stopping on the next to the last step. As soon as he spoke, Rollo abandoned his harrying of Earlene and William and dashed up the steps, a couple higher than Mr. Potter, and jumped on him from behind. Mr. Potter stumbled down the last steps, and swatted at the dog with an open hand. "Drat that dog. Get off," he commanded, but Rollo followed him down the stairs, whining and wagging, and jumped on him again. The terrier's enthusiasm brought Jack and Emily Ann onto the scene, willing to join in the fun. Then Jack saw Ambrose still kneeling on the floor with his towel, and ran over to nuzzle Ambrose behind the ear.

"Hey, you old Jack rabbit," Ambrose said, catching hold of Jack's collar. "Come on, you can help me dry up any more drips." He rose gracefully, walked around Mr. Potter, and started up the stairs, swabbing now and then when he saw a wet place.

"Oh, Mr. Potter," I said. "Apparently there was a mishap with the bridge and Miss Mason nearly went into the lake. She's upstairs getting dry. We'll find out more in a moment."

He was still pushing Rollo away. "I do not understand why they left their dog down here, then," he said. "Normally I am fond of dogs, but this one is a confounded nuisance."

"Nonsense, Potter," said William, coming over to snag Rollo. "You should be flattered by his attention.

176

You seem to be the only person in the house he really likes." He looked down at his hairy bundle. "Is that right, Rollo? Are you just a friendly little Toto kind of guy?" Rollo struggled, straining toward Mr. Potter, but William grasped him firmly.

Ambrose's voice floated down the stairwell; he and Jack had made the turn at the landing. A woman answered, Miss Gray I thought, then their footsteps sounded on the stairs.

"Oh, good, here they come," I said. Miss Mason and Miss Gray came into view, stripped of their wraps and wearing jeans and heavy sweaters. Ambrose followed a step or two behind. "Let's go in the living room," I said. "Miss Mason, are you all right?"

"I'm fine," she said, reaching the hallway. "Just cold still. And somewhat shaken."

"Kay has the kettle on," I said, shepherding the group into the adjoining room, where there was enough seating for everyone. "Let me go make some tea for us all, and then you can tell us what happened. Unless you would prefer coffee."

"Tea would be great," she said, sounding a bit wan. I settled her in an overstuffed chair and tucked an afghan around her, then hurried to the kitchen. Kay was there, buttering slices of toasted brioche. A large earthenware pot was warming next to the stove. I picked up a piece of toast and she slapped at my hand, but I managed to bite into it before she got it away from me.

"You are my most favorite cousin in the whole world," I told her. I reached for the knife and cut two

177

more slices of the rich bread and gave it to her to toast.

"Well, thanks," she said, "though the compliment pales a little since I'm your only cousin in the whole world. Is everything okay out there? Who was in the office? What the hell is Doris doing here? And is the woman who fell in the lake okay? I thought she might need a bit more than a cup of tea. What's going on?"

"I have got so much to tell you," I said, thinking of the Pan figurine hiding in plain sight across the room. I considered showing it to her now, but I was afraid she'd scream and bring people running. Since I didn't know how it had gotten into the office, I didn't want to possibly alert the wrong people that I had found it. "Let's find out what happened to Miss Mason first. Is that water hot yet?"

She pulled the lid from the kettle and peered in. "Just about," she said, and turned to butter the two pieces of toast as they popped up. "Is there a tray or something to put this stuff on?"

"Sure." I went to fetch the cart from the butler's pantry. I wheeled it into the kitchen and loaded on the plate of toast and the tea pot, along with cream and sugar, spoons and napkins. The lower shelf was already stacked with small plates and an assortment of cups and saucers, in anticipation of serving afternoon tea. Steam started pouring in earnest from the kettle's spout, so Kay grabbed a potholder and hefted it over the pot, releasing that wonderful tea smell as the bubbling water hit the leaves. When she was done I took the kettle from her and refilled it, then set it on the stove to heat. To her questioning look I said, "If everyone wants tea, we'll need to refill the pot in a few minutes. Come on, let's find out what happened to Miss Mason."

18

I pushed the cart through the butler's pantry to the dining room, then into the living room. Everyone was there. Miss Mason remained cocooned inside the wool afghan, and Miss Gray sat cross-legged on the floor next to her. She had her fingers around Rollo's collar; he was trying to get to Mr. Potter, but when Kay and I arrived he turned instead to bark at us.

Mr. Potter and Earlene were in the two wing chairs flanking the fireplace, where Ambrose was putting the finishing touches on a fire he had started. It crackled and popped a couple of times, and a spark hit the fire screen as he set it in place. Jack had been helping him, and now he lay down on the hearthrug. Earlene's feet were several inches off the floor, and she had crammed some decorative pillows behind her back. Mr. Potter sat stiffly erect. He wasn't quite snarling at Rollo, but the suggestion was there in the set of his lips.

Doris, William, and Emily Ann were on the sofa. William had an arm around Doris's shoulders, and with the other hand was stroking Emily Ann's sleek head. Both were leaning on him.

Ambrose came to help with the cart. We positioned it near the archway into the foyer, and he poured a cup of tea which he conveyed to Miss Mason, along with the plate of toast. Hot tea and toast are my family's cure-all for any accident or illness.

As Ambrose murmured a question to Miss Mason about sugar or lemon, I looked around the room. I felt like a famous detective in a novel, all my suspects gathered before me to hear my brilliant recitation of how the crime had been committed and by whom. Within the next half hour, one of them would cry out, "I did it, and I'm glad!" Except that not only was I no detective, I wasn't even sure what the crime was. Other than harboring a stolen porcelain figurine, that is, and I was hardly in a position to point a dramatic finger at any of the assembled group and say sternly, "You stole my mother's Pan!" My fantasy concluded with the famous detective being hauled off to the loony bin, locked up in a padded room, and the key thrown away. Which at the moment did have a certain appeal. I sank down on the nearest empty sofa.

Kay handed me a cup of tea and sat down beside me. I wished I had brought along another slice of toast. This was no doubt the kind of food I would get in that imagined mental hospital. I could get a head start by practicing on it now.

I took a deep breath and became the innkeeper again. "Help yourselves to tea, everyone. Miss Mason, when you feel up to it, please tell us what happened at the bridge."

She took a sip from the cup Ambrose had given her. "Carolyn and I had been out with Rollo and Jack for maybe an hour, and we were circling back to come in and warm up. We'd been playing in the woods with them, and we came out near the bridge. Rollo ran out on the bridge. He didn't want to come when I called him—"

Mr. Potter made an inaudible comment. She looked at him inquiringly, then went on.

"I didn't have any treats left in my pocket to lure him back. So I stepped onto the bridge to grab him, and he dashed by me back to Carolyn. Then as I turned around to follow him, the bridge gave a kind of lurch. The right edge was lower than the left and the surface was pretty slick, and I scrambled forward and tried to jump back to land. That's when the whole thing gave way and went crashing into the lake. One of my feet ended up in the water and I was about to fall in, but Caro grabbed my hand and pulled me up. Oh my god, that water is *cold*."

"So the ice didn't hold?" I asked, hoping that the bridge was still lying on top of the frozen part of the lake and we could somehow grab it and reattach it to its moorings. Both women shook their heads.

"The ice totally gave way, and then the bridge went under," Miss Gray said. "I didn't think the lake was so deep there, but you know how this winter has been— plenty of rain and not much freezing weather."

William was at the cart getting tea for his bride. He handed Doris the cup. As he sat back down he said,

"I know you needed to hurry back to the house, but did you notice what gave way?"

Miss Mason shook her head. "I didn't even look. It sounds wimpy now, but that water was like being stabbed. All I could think of was getting away from there."

Miss Gray added, "The rings that the bridge hooks to were still there. That's all I noticed."

William went on, "Was anyone else around?" I wondered if he too had seen himself in the role of famous detective.

"I didn't notice anyone, did you?" Carolyn Gray said, looking at her companion. "And Rollo wasn't barking," she added.

To my mind this was a convincing argument.

Kay stirred beside me. "What about footprints in the snow?"

The two women looked at each other, then Miss Gray shook her head. "There were a bunch. Nothing struck me as unusual. And when Georgina's foot went into the water, it splashed up on the bank. I suppose it could have erased some footprints. The way it's still snowing, though, there won't be any left to see before long."

I looked out the window. She was right; it was snowing harder than ever.

"We'd better get out there and see what we're dealing with," I said. "Ambrose, will you come with me and Kay?" Looking around at the assembled guests, I added, "We'll be back as quickly as we can and let you know how it looks."

Kay and I rose from our sofa, and Ambrose straightened from the stance he had taken near the fireplace. William stood as well.

"Let me come along," he said. "I'm a useful kind of guy in emergencies."

"Sure," I said, figuring that if there was any chance of hauling the bridge out of the water, we'd need some muscle power. "Get your coat and meet us at the car."

The drive from the house to the bridge was nearly impossible. In less than an hour, since Earlene and I had arrived at the house, our tracks had been obliterated. The day was darker as well, and the winding drive to the bridge, so pleasantly curved on a sunny day, now became an obstacle course taking all my concentration.

"Good thing there aren't any ditches along the drive," William commented as I pulled out of a skid that banged the back left side of the car against a snow-covered bush. "Those are always fun to slide into."

I didn't reply; I was too busy trying to remember if in fact there were any ditches beside the drive. Logically I knew that it wouldn't be a disaster if there were; even if the car were disabled, we were all warmly dressed and could walk back to the house. Though snowing hard, this was not the kind of blizzard that would obliterate the world, where we would have to run a rope from the house to the barn so we could feed the animals. I felt a little better at the realization I had no barn or animals, other than a trio of dogs, to be responsible for. Only a houseful of people with widely varying temperaments, and one with the measles. Which made me realize that I had forgotten about Terry.

"I forgot all about Terry," I said aloud.

"Who's Terry?" Kay and William said in chorus.

"I looked in on him before we left," Ambrose said. "He'd fallen asleep in front of the computer. We'll have to get him into bed as soon as we get back."

"Who's Terry?" Kay asked again.

"He's my housekeeping help," I said. I kept my eyes focused on where I was attempting to drive. "He called me yesterday to say he couldn't come to work because he has the measles—"

"The measles!" she exclaimed. "Wouldn't he be a little old for the measles?"

"His mother home-schooled him until high school," Ambrose said, "so perhaps he was never exposed to the normal childhood diseases."

"It sounds to me like he wasn't exposed to any common sense, either," Kay said. "What in the world is he doing at the house if he has the measles? I'm assuming Louisa didn't offer to play nurse."

Kay knows my reluctance to tend to the sick, which has nothing to do with anything that happened to me at camp and everything to do with marrying a man who was simultaneously infantile and tyrannical when he had the slightest ailment.

"He snuck out of his house and rode over here on a Vespa to retrieve a project from Mary Pat's computer for Mr. Pearlman's social studies class," I told her. "It's due on Wednesday—"

185

"Mr. Pearlman?" she broke in. "Our Mr. Pearlman? Geez, he must be a million years old." She shook her head. "No wonder the kid had to get his project."

We were silent, three of us in the car remembering the long, long hours we had spent in Mr. Pearlman's class, though not, I am afraid, any of the information he had attempted to instill in us. He was probably the teacher responsible for not teaching me that the Secret Service is in charge of investigating counterfeiting. The man was so intensely boring that I used to think he could be used as a secret weapon. Place him on a battlefield with thousands of enemy troops, and he would have them begging for mercy and crying to surrender in no time.

We slid into the area by the floating bridge, spun a little as I braked. I sucked in my breath as the car neared the lake, then whooshed out as we came to a stop. The four of us got out of the car.

Before we approached the bridge, I looked around for footprints that might tell us something, but everything had been covered by the heavy snow. The suggestion of dips here and there could be changes in the terrain as easily as places someone had walked earlier. William led the way to the bank overlooking the lake.

The floating bridge had vanished. Gray water heaved between the island and the mainland. In the parking lot on the other side, the three cars belonging to the inn's guests were so heaped with snow as to be mere lumps, and even Ambrose's Mercedes and Earlene's SUV were well on their way to becoming matching lumps. The bridge was no longer attached on the far side either.

William and Ambrose went to the edge of the water and peered into its murky depths. "Must be deep here," William said. "I don't see a thing."

"Could that be the end of the bridge?" Ambrose said, pointing. I went over and looked.

"Could be," I said. "Of course it could be a rock, too."

"Is there any other way off the island?" William asked.

I shook my head. "Not that I know of. Ambrose?"

"Mary Pat might have a canoe or something, but I have no idea where or even if she does. I've seen her swim but never known her to use a boat," he said.

"How the hell did this happen?" Kay wanted to know.

I looked at the cement landing, which had two hefty I-bolts solidly imbedded in it. "Could it be related to the weather? The snow made the clips retract and come loose?" It sounded ridiculous. I was grasping at straws.

"There's no way to know for sure until we can retrieve the bridge and take a look at it," William said. "But I'm betting on human intervention."

A cold chill went down my back that had nothing to do with any snow that might have landed on my neck. "Someone stranded us here on purpose?" My voice rose in a squeak. "Who would do such a thing? And why?"

"Yeah," said Kay. "And was it done from the mainland side, or from here?"

19

The icy piano of George Winston's *December* CD met us at the door when we returned to the house. Ambrose, Kay and I went into the kitchen to take off our wraps, and William headed upstairs to his room. I checked the time—going on one o'clock. The toast I had consumed earlier had been a mere bite and I felt a little lightheaded from hunger. Not only did I need to eat, but so did the other nine people in the house.

"Good lord," I said, "I've got to feed everyone."

I must have looked aghast. Kay said immediately, "Ambrose and I will help you fix lunch."

"Thanks," I managed, thinking again she was the best cousin in the world.

"What kind of supplies do you have?" Ambrose asked.

"We're fine on bread right now," I said, "and there are several kinds of cheese. How about if we put out stuff to make sandwiches, and people can put together what they like. But then we'd better take stock of what we have, because obviously we're going to be here at least a couple of days."

Ambrose nodded, looking out the window. "No one is going to get down that drive and boat over here until the snow stops."

"Right. And the food on hand was intended for breakfasts, not three meals a day for ten people."

I heard footsteps on the back stairs. Earlene appeared, carrying my bucket of cleaning supplies.

"Welcome back," she said. "All the beds are made and the bathrooms are good enough for anyone. How did the bridge look?"

"Oh, Earlene, you didn't!" I exclaimed, and at the same moment Kay said, "Bridge? What bridge?"

"That bad?"

"No sign of the bridge," Ambrose put in. "It's gone."

"Well." She thought for a moment, then said, "In that case, I guess I'll finally get to spend a night at the Bunny Farm Inn. My sister Gina will be so jealous. We always talked about going to a bed and breakfast sometime. Louisa, may I use your phone to let them know I'm staying out here? I left my cell phone in the car. I figured I'd only be here for a few minutes."

"Of course," I said, gesturing to the kitchen phone. "Help yourself."

Kay turned to the fridge as Earlene picked up the receiver. She listened for a moment, then pushed buttons several times. "Louisa, this phone doesn't seem to be working."

"What?" I went over and took the receiver, but I knew as soon as I put it to my ear that it was dead. "The storm must have downed a line somewhere."

"Use my cell phone," Kay offered. "It's in my purse there hanging on that chair."

I reached into the purse, but my hand didn't feel anything like a phone. Frowning, I set the purse on the table and went through it methodically, but there was no phone there. I looked up with a grin. "Kay," I teased her, "I don't want to hear anything more about me forgetting to carry my phone with me."

She frowned and slammed the fridge door. "What are you talking about? I never forget my phone."

I had to admit that I had never known her to be without it. "You weren't using it just before you left home? Maybe you laid it down somewhere."

"No," she said decisively, "it was in my purse. That's where I keep the red one. Here, let me look."

She emptied the contents of her bag onto the table. No tiny red phone.

"I don't think we can blame this one on the weather," I said.

"All right, but let's not jump to conclusions," Ambrose said. "Kay, unlikely as it seems, it is possible that you didn't put your phone in your purse—"

"I don't put it there, I keep it there," she insisted.

"It could have disappeared before we came out here," he went on. "Maybe someone at the store snagged it. Earlene, was anyone in the kitchen while we were gone?"

"Any of them could have been," she said. "When you went to check the bridge, I figured it would be a good chance to get their rooms tidied. I knew Louisa hadn't had a chance to do it yet. So I told them I was going up to take care of the housekeeping. They all stayed down here. Someone put on that music. They're probably still in the living room. Oh, except that Mr.

190

Potter. He came upstairs and asked how long I would be. I was just finishing his room so I told him I was done and I think he's up there now."

"Well, someone's sure to have a phone you can use," I told her. "We'll go find out. Oh, and we need to make lunch, and figure out where to put Terry to bed..." My voice trailed off. I felt pulled in so many directions at once that I couldn't move at all.

"All right, you and Earlene go find a phone," Kay said decisively, "and Ambrose and I will put together lunch. When Earlene has made her call, we should call the sheriff or someone to report the bridge disappearing, so bring the phone in here."

When Kay takes command, I obey. So does everyone else, with the possible exception of her on-again, off-again chief of police boyfriend Ed. Earlene and I went through the dining room to the small parlor, but no one was there. I turned to the living room. I heard Rollo bark, so I knew I was on the right track. Doris, Miss Mason and Miss Gray were where we had left them, and William was putting logs on the fire. Rollo barked at me from the sofa where Doris was sitting. She looked sideways at him with an expression that would have quelled a hostile witness, but had no discernible effect on the terrier. Emily Ann lay between Miss Gray and the fire, basking in warmth and being petted at the same time. Jack peered out from under a table in the corner. He thumped his tail at me but did not get up.

William straightened and dusted off his hands. "There, that ought to keep burning for a while," he said.

"Thanks," I said. "Listen, does anyone have a cell phone we can borrow? The house phone seems to be out, probably because of the storm."

All four of them said, at the same time, "I have one." I thought to myself, cell phone stocks must be a great investment.

"Are they upstairs?" I asked. They all nodded.

"I'll go get one of ours," said William, heading for the stairs.

When he was gone I asked Miss Mason, "Are you okay? Have you thawed out? I'm so glad you didn't get hurt."

She nodded. "I'm fine. Did you see the bridge?"

I shook my head. "I'm afraid there's no bridge to see."

Doris spoke from across the room. "But how are we going to get out of here?"

I looked at her. "We're not, for the moment. Even if the bridge were there, the snow has gotten so deep that Earlene's SUV is probably the only vehicle out there that could move, and I'm not sure about it. But the bridge was the only way I know of to get off this island, so after Earlene phones her family to tell them she's okay, we'll be calling the sheriff to let them know we're stranded out here."

William's voice drifted down from upstairs. "Doris, where did you put your phone?"

"It's in my overnight case," she called back.

"I looked there. Where else could it be?"

She stood up and headed for the stairs. "Men," she said as she went, shaking her head. "They can never find anything."

But in a few minutes they were both back. "Our phones are gone," William said. "We looked everywhere."

Miss Gray rose from the floor in a single lithe movement that I couldn't have managed even a child. "Gosh, I hope ours are there." She hurried from the room, and I heard her footsteps ascending the stairs. She too was back in a few minutes, a grim expression on her usually pleasant face. "No phones," she reported. "This obviously is not a coincidence."

"No," I said, "I don't think so."

Ambrose appeared in the doorway that led to the dining room. "We've put out some lunch, so whenever you are hungry just come and help yourselves." He looked around at everyone's glum faces. "What's the matter?"

"All of our phones are missing," William spoke for the group.

"All right," I said, "we'll search the house. They have to be somewhere. Let's eat something first, and then we'll start looking."

There were murmurs of agreement, and everyone headed for the dining room. I suddenly remembered Mr. Potter. "I'll go up and tell Mr. Potter. And maybe he has a phone," I said.

I cut through the kitchen and took the back stairs. I stopped for a moment in my room, closed the door, and stood with my eyes closed and my mind blank. The only coherent thought in my head sounded suspiciously like "Everything that can go wrong will go wrong."

Being alone was a respite I allowed myself for only a minute. Taking a deep breath, I left my room and continued down the hall and around the corner to Mr. Potter's room. I knocked on his door and called, "Mr. Potter?"

"Just a moment." I heard some small noises, indistinguishable as to origin, and then he opened the door. "Yes?"

"We've put some things out in the dining room for lunch," I told him, thinking uncharitably that maybe Mr. Potter had taken out the bridge so that I would be forced to provide him with lunch and dinner. "Come down and help yourself whenever you're hungry. And I was wondering if you have a cell phone I could borrow. The house phone is out, I imagine due to the weather."

"You mean you don't have one?" he grumbled. "I think it would be a good idea to have one when running a business."

"I do, but I'm not sure where I put it. I would really appreciate it if I could borrow yours."

"Oh, all right. Just a moment." He left the door open and I watched as he crossed to the overnight case sitting on the table in the corner. He rummaged inside, taking out objects and laying them in rows on the table. At last he stopped and looked around. "I was sure I had left it here. Maybe it's in a coat pocket."

He went to the closet and opened the door, which put him out of my view. In a moment he popped his head around the door, scowling. "It's not here. My phone is missing. What is the meaning of this?" he demanded.

I sighed. "Not yours too. Everyone's phones have disappeared."

He slammed the closet door and stalked towards me. "Someone has been looting our possessions," he snarled. "That woman who was up here who said she was doing the housekeeping. She was in all our rooms. It was her."

His tirade surprised a laugh out of me. "Earlene?" I said. "It could not possibly have been Earlene."

His face turned an alarming shade of red. "Of course it could," he insisted. "She was here. I saw her in my room."

"You saw her making your bed and checking your towel supply." I didn't feel like laughing any more. "Earlene is my friend, and her reputation is impeccable."

"Or it could have been that teenager in the office," he went on. "The one getting into the computer."

"What were you doing in the office?" I asked him. "That door was closed."

He didn't answer my question. "Kids like that steal things to sell. They take drugs, you know."

I was seized with a longing to kick this guy out of the inn. Unfortunately, he was snowed in along with the rest of us. Of course, pushing him out into the snow might have a beneficial cooling effect, as well as getting him out of my face. I took a deep breath.

"Terry has worked here for some time, and I have never known of any complaint about him," I said in my coldest voice. I love to tell the truth. No need to mention I'd never even heard of Terry before a few days ago, and had seen him only once for a couple of minutes. "We will search for the phones later. If you want some lunch, come down when you're ready." I turned on my heel and marched away. I needed to get something to eat before Mr. Potter came downstairs, because I knew that being in the same room with him would be sure to take my appetite away.

20

The rest of Saturday became a blur of activity. We got through a lunch where everyone except Mr. Potter participated in getting-to-know-you-better conversation. Even Kay and Doris managed to be civil to each other.

Mr. Potter came down after everyone else had left the table, made himself a sandwich and returned to his room. Probably to scatter spiteful crumbs for me to clean up. I hope the crumbs might bring out playful mice to keep him awake in the night.

Kay made up the daybed in the maid's room next to the kitchen for Terry and tucked him in while Ambrose put out lunch. Then Ambrose sat with the fever-ish boy until Terry fell into a fitful sleep. Kay and I repaired to the kitchen after lunch, where I became obsessed with whether I had enough food for everyone. I looked through all the cupboards, then said, "At our current rate of consumption, we will have nothing to eat except granola by Monday afternoon."

"Louisa! How long do you think we're going to be here?" Kay exclaimed. "Someone is bound to miss us and come by soon. All we need is a boat to get out of here." She was using her practical voice on me.

"Who's going to miss us?" I asked her. "Bob is still in San Francisco and won't be back till late Tuesday. You aren't speaking to Ed, so how likely is it he'll be looking for you?"

She gave a reluctant nod. "Pretty unlikely, unless his mother convinces him to invite me over for dinner so she can freeze me in a snow bank."

"Ambrose said that George is on duty all weekend, and with the storm he'll be working around the clock helping stranded motorists. Cleta knew you were coming out here and she'll just assume you stayed because of the weather. Maybe someone will be looking for Terry, but I bet his mother thinks he's at his granny's and vice versa, and they probably wouldn't look here for him. Unless there's some kind of miracle I don't think we'll get out of here before Wednesday morning at the earliest. And that's assuming it ever stops snowing."

"I still don't think we'll run out of food," Kay insisted.

"How long do you think two dozen eggs will last ten people? And two cans of tomatoes, and a three pound brick of cheddar?" I asked her.

Her eyes widened. "Is that all we've got? I see what you mean," she said. "So, how much granola is there?"

I had to admit that there was a lot of granola. Mary Pat ordered it in bulk and had recently received a fresh shipment. So we wouldn't actually become the

Donner party. But there were a lot of meals to be responsible for between now and being rescued.

I badly wanted to take a nap and not deal with any of this.

Then there were the phones. While I was mixing another batch of bread, Mr. Potter came stumping into the kitchen and wanted to know when we were going to search the house for his cell phone. I wanted to scream at him that no one cared about his stupid phone, but it appeared that I was the only person in the house who didn't feel naked without one. So I asked Kay to spearhead the search effort. She called all the guests together and divided them into teams to search each room. As a way of passing a snowy afternoon, it was probably as good as any other. I thought about asking everyone to wield a dust cloth while they were going through their allotted rooms, but decided against it.

Mr. Potter wanted to start his search in the kitchen. I suddenly thought of the Pan sitting on the Welsh dresser among the teapots. "No," I said firmly. "I will be at work in there. I'll search this room myself."

"How do we know you aren't the one who took the phones?" the annoying man said. A look I could only describe as speaking passed between Miss Mason and Miss Gray, but I couldn't tell what it was saying.

Kay drew herself up to her full five foot two. "Mr. Potter," she said coldly, "if you knew anything about my cousin, you would know that the last item in the world she would *ever* steal is a telephone, let alone six of them. The kitchen is off limits. Let's go." They went. But their search turned up not a single phone.

I spent the afternoon cooking, between interruptions from Kay and Ambrose and various guests, as well as my own periodic checks on Terry. When I put everything on the sideboard, I was a little startled at the menu I had prepared. There was a long glass casserole dish of lasagna, and a steaming bowl of fluffy mashed potatoes, and another casserole of macaroni and cheese, and French green beans with almond slivers, and a loaf of freshly baked bread. I hoped there would be enough to feed everyone. I was not accustomed to making food for more than a couple of people.

Doris came into the dining room on William's arm. "Oh, good," she said, looking at the collation. "We're dining on comfort food. I bet there's cheesecake or apple pie for dessert."

"Perhaps you would like to take over in the kitchen?" I glared at her.

"Doris, behave," said her husband. "This looks delicious. I'll take your share if you don't want it."

She bumped him aside with her hip and helped herself to lasagna and green beans.

After dinner no one wanted to go to their rooms. Even Mr. Potter seated himself by the fire and read a book, or pretended to. Kay had found some cards during the phone search, and she and Ambrose took on all comers at poker, everyone playing for fantastic and completely imaginary stakes. I stayed in the kitchen, washing the dishes, putting yet another batch of bread to rise for breakfast, wiping imaginary crumbs off the counters. From time to time I checked on Terry, who still slept fitfully, twitching and grinding his teeth. I sat on the rocker in his room and watched him for a bit, feeling drained and a bit depressed.

The entire day had gone by and I had never found a chance to tell Kay about the Pan figurine. It was only a quarter till nine, and I wanted nothing so much as to fall asleep. But my role in the house was that of hostess, and I had next to no experience with this kind of house party. Roger and I had seldom had overnight guests, and he was often away from home. I had far more experience at, and inclination for, being alone.

Besides, when you read about house parties, usually in a cozy English murder mystery, a horde of servants are on hand to smooth the details of living. There is plenty of food, and a chauffeur to take one to the train if one needs to leave, and the hostess has ample leisure to don a glamorous silk dress for dinner. I had a houseful of people, most of whom I'd known only a couple of days, who had little in common with each other. I was stranded on an island, the bridge had disappeared, several feet of snow blanketed the ground, and we had no way to communicate with the outside world. I was also encumbered with a teenage boy with the measles, and a small dog who barked at everything.

In the plus column, I had about fifty pounds of granola in the kitchen and a batch of bread rising.

As I stood to leave Terry's room, I recalled that I had one other asset so often employed in those English mysteries.

201

I had tea. I didn't have a housekeeper in black bombazine, whatever the hell bombazine was, to brew it for me, but I did have tea.

I returned to the kitchen and put the kettle on. When it was whistling merrily, I selected a small pot from the Welsh dresser, making a face at the Pan as I did so. He ignored me. I spooned tea into the pot and filled it. While it brewed I sliced bread left from dinner and made toast—the piece I'd had before lunch had reminded me how much I like it. Then I sat at the table and ate my hot buttered toast and drank the tea into which I had put some brown sugar and a little cream.

Comfort food indeed.

Refreshed, I refilled the kettle and selected a much larger teapot. When the new pot was ready, I put it on the cart and slipped over it a tea cozy knitted of fluffy yarn that probably came from the former residents of the Bunny Farm. I put the last of the cookies that Kay and Ambrose had been eating earlier in the day on a plate and made sure there were enough cups and saucers. Then I wheeled the cart into the dining room where the party was still going strong.

The folding card table in the hall closet had not been large enough to accommodate all the players. I found Kay and Ambrose, William and Doris, Miss Mason and Miss Gray, and Earlene all at the dining table, in the same chairs where they had eaten dinner.

"I've brought you some tea," I announced. "Who's winning?"

Earlene beamed. "Well, I'm up more than three million dollars."

"Earlene, I believe you cheat," William groaned. She laughed merrily at him.

"These cards just have an affinity for women," said Kay. "I'll be able to open a chain of shops with what I've won so far."

Miss Mason snorted. "Speak for yourself. I'm going to have to go into indentured servitude if I keep getting the same kind of hands. Or else get into that counterfeiting business we were talking about at breakfast."

Doris tut-tutted. "I don't know about that," she said. "From what I heard in Las Vegas, counterfeiting and gambling do not make a healthy combination. The newspaper was running a series of stories while we were there and it sounded like passing bad paper in Vegas is a really risky business. The articles read like a movie script about the mafia."

"Chopping off fingers so you can't do it again?" Kay asked with ghoulish glee.

"Yeah," said Doris, her face deadpan. "Chopping off fingers, both before and after they kill you."

Mr. Potter made a disgusted noise and rose from his chair by the fire, leaving the room without a word.

"Sounds even worse than innkeeping," I said.

The gamblers all laughed as though they thought I was joking.

"Well, help yourselves to tea and cookies," I told them. "I'm heading upstairs. Kay, could you look in on Terry from time to time? Call me if he looks any worse."

"Sure," she said. "I'll be up in a little while."

I called Emily Ann and Jack. They accompanied me through the kitchen. From the dining room fresh laughter erupted and followed us up the stairs.

21

Kay and I were sharing Mary Pat's suite. Short of spending the night in the attic, it was the only way I could accommodate everyone. I'd given Earlene my room, and Ambrose would sleep next door to her in the last available upstairs bedroom. Terry was still in the maid's room next to the kitchen. That left either the sofas downstairs or Mary Pat's space for Kay and me.

Mary Pat's private area was frankly luxurious—a long room that might originally have been two. She had arranged a sitting area near the door to the hall with a couple of love seats, a large square coffee table, and a television and DVD player in the corner. Her private bathroom featured an oversized shower head suspended above an old fashioned tub. The bathing experience was not unlike being caught in a spring shower. At the other end of the room, her king size bed was covered with a satin comforter and half a dozen large pillows.

I had been reluctant to invade Mary Pat's suite, but I didn't see how she could reasonably object. I couldn't call and ask her. I imagined miraculously finding one of the missing phones and calling Mary Pat in England to tell her that we were snowed in and the bridge was gone and we were going to run out of food and Terry had the measles and there were ten people in the house and oh, by the way, could my cousin and I sleep in her bed?

As I brushed my teeth, I thought about the missing phones. Many times in the past few years (when I'd nearly been rammed by drivers chatting as they drove, or been shopping and had to listen to someone idiotically talking away in a store, or had a quiet dinner in a restaurant invaded by someone's phone call) I'd wanted to make all the cell phones in the world disappear. And the first time I really needed one they were gone.

I climbed into bed wondering about the inn's cell phone. I still had no idea when I had last seen it, but assumed it had been spirited away with the rest of them.

I read for a few minutes, then when my eyelids grew heavy I turned off the light. And immediately was wide awake again. A grainy black and white movie began to unreel in my brain, in which the Pan figurine came to life and prowled the house, stealing cell phones. He was still at his nefarious deeds when Kay came quietly in the door. I closed my eyes and pretended to be asleep as she slid into bed beside me. Her snores began in about three minutes. The house was quiet, everyone must be in bed. I slid into sleep.

Rollo barked. My eyes flew open. I was surprised to see the clock read a little after three. I was sure I had only dozed off a moment before. He barked again. I shook my head to clear it. Jack snuffled at the door as he had done the night before, while Emily Ann stood guard at Kay's side of the bed. Kay snored on.

I scrambled out of bed and hurried across the room. When I opened the door, Jack flew down the back stairs. Just like last night. Again we ended up in front of the office door. I hesitated a moment, hoping the boogeyman wouldn't jump out at me. Or even the boogeymouse. But the dogs were there to save me, so I turned the knob and threw the door open.

Jack and Emily Ann erupted into the room. I was surprised to see the desk lamp glowing, and once more the computer was on. The small upholstered wing chair that usually stood under the slant of the ceiling where the stairs rose had been moved about three feet into the room. Jack brought his questing nose to that part of the room and searched along the baseboard where the chair normally sat, deeply interested in some scent.

Footsteps thudded in the hall behind me. I turned to see Ambrose and Miss Mason. "What's going on?" Ambrose asked. His graying blond hair was standing up in spikes and he his eyelids looked thick with sleep.

Miss Mason held Rollo. "I'm so sorry he barked," she bleated. "I can't believe he woke everyone up again."

Rollo wiggled in her arms, and she set him down. He ran into the office and joined Jack, who was still patrolling the area under the stairs. After giving the baseboards a good sniff, Rollo started to bark and jump. I went to the dogs and crouched down to see if I could figure out what they were interested in. Jack broke off his hunting and came to be petted, and Rollo stopped bouncing off the wall and backed up to bark at me. With a bitten-off exclamation, Miss Mason grabbed the terrier, and I nudged Jack out of my line of sight.

I couldn't see anything unusual about that portion of the wall. Like the rest of the wainscoting in the room it was paneled in beautiful oak, with a chair rail and wide moldings at the top and bottom. I looked over my shoulder at Ambrose.

"Could you point the desk lamp over here?" I requested. He did so. I pushed up onto my feet and moved back, but various dogs kept getting in my way, so I invited Jack and Emily Ann into the hall and shut the door on them. I heard one of them, probably Jack, flop down in front of the door to sniff at the crack. Then Ambrose and I went back over to the section of wall spotlighted by the desk lamp.

We couldn't see a darned thing out of the ordinary.

I reached over and rapped on it in several places with my knuckles.

"They all sound the same to me," said Miss Mason from beside the desk, where she held Rollo in a tight grip."

"And perfectly solid." I shook my head. "I have no idea what's going on. Someone's been in here again, unless desk lights and computers have evolved to the point where they can turn themselves on at will."

"What do you mean, 'again?'" Ambrose asked. I realized I hadn't told him and Kay about the other interesting events of my sojourn at the Bunny Farm Inn.

"We did this last night too," I told him. "Rollo barked, Jack got all excited, I followed him down here and there was nothing to be seen. William and I checked the whole downstairs and didn't find anything. I haven't seen any evidence of mice, but it *is* an old house and there's plenty of room in the walls for them. Something like that might interest the dogs."

If Miss Mason hadn't been standing there I would have told him about finding her in here on Friday morning.

He ran a hand over his rumpled hair. "We should check the place again. Maybe someone couldn't sleep and decided to play computer games, but let's take a look."

I turned to Miss Mason. "We can handle this. You should go back to bed."

"Oh, okay." She looked a little surprised. "I'll take Rollo back up. I'm about to tape his mouth shut, if he won't stop barking."

"Maybe he's gotten it out of his system now," I said, though I tried to remember where I had seen a roll of duct tape. I went to the desk and logged off the computer, turned off the desk lamp, and followed the others out of the room, clicking off the light before I closed the door. Miss Mason headed right and went up the stairs.

"Let's peek in on Terry," I said, "and then check through the downstairs." Ambrose nodded.

We walked the few steps to the end of the hall and around the corner to Terry's room. Ambrose knocked lightly on the door. No answer. "He must have slept through it all," he murmured, and opened the door. We had left a small, shaded lamp burning on the table in the corner, and in its dim light we could see that the rumpled bed was unoccupied.

"Good grief," Ambrose said. "Where the hell is that boy? Tell me he hasn't decided in a fever delirium to ride his Vespa home."

"He couldn't have," I said, more confidently than I felt. "And where are the dogs?" I added, for they had not been in the hall when we left the office. We looked at each other and hurried out of Terry's room.

"You go that way, I'll go this," Ambrose said, pointing. I checked the bathroom across the hall from Terry's room, then went along the hall past the office and flicked on the light in the library. No one there. Across the entry to the living room, where a small lamp on a corner table gave a cozy glow. No Terry, no dogs. The dining room too was empty, but at last I found our quarry in the small parlor. Ambrose was already there, looking down at the disheveled figure wrapped in an afghan, asleep on the sofa. Jack and Emily Ann sat beside him, and a book lay on the floor where he had dropped it.

"He must have gotten bored and decided to get up," Ambrose whispered.

"Could he have been in the office?" I whispered back. "He does seem pretty obsessed with his paper for Mr. Pearlman."

Ambrose shrugged. "Could have, I guess, but then what was Rollo barking at and what was Jack looking for? And why was the chair moved?"

Terry stirred in his sleep, then quieted.

"Maybe whoever was in there dropped something and it rolled under the chair and they moved it. And Rollo could have been barking at anything. Or nothing. But Jack...Jack is pretty reliable."

Jack looked up at the sound of his name and thumped the carpet with his tail.

"True," Ambrose nodded, "but he is a dog, after all. He would probably think something like that mouse you mentioned is important."

"I'm going to put a padlock on that office door," I snarled. "Everyone's been in there. Terry, Miss Mason, Mr. Potter—"

My voice must have risen, because Terry stirred and opened his eyes. "Where am I?" he mumbled.

"You fell asleep on the sofa" Ambrose said. "Come on, buddy, let me help you back to bed."

Terry sat up, pushing the afghan aside, and Ambrose reached down and pulled him up by his hand. "Hey," Ambrose said, and put the back of his hand on Terry's forehead. "Your fever has gone down. You're a lot cooler than the last time I looked in on you."

"Oh, good," Terry mumbled, "I always, like, wanted to be cool."

Ambrose laughed. "You are better if you're making puns. Come on, back to your room. And don't scratch those spots, young man."

211

Ambrose led Terry off. I folded the afghan and followed them. When Terry was settled, we headed up the back stairs. Ambrose closed the door on his room, and I shooed the dogs into Mary Pat's suite. Kay's snoring was the only sound in the dark room. The familiar noise was comforting, and she had kept the bed warm while I was downstairs. Soon I drifted into an exhausted sleep.

Until Rollo barked.

This time I barely had my eyes open when I hit the floor. Again the dogs were at the door, but when I opened it they turned toward the front of the house, instead of charging down the back stairs. I found them surrounding Mr. Potter, a few feet from the front staircase with his back to the wall.

Rollo's bark was cut short. I heard one of his owners hissing at him to Be Quiet. I imagined she had her hand clamped around his little muzzle. As I opened my mouth to speak to Mr. Potter, the door to the nearest room flew open to reveal Doris, wearing tailored silk pajamas in midnight blue with yellow piping. Her expression was grim. When Mr. Potter caught sight of her he looked abashed.

She said nothing, just breathed in and out at us a few times, and then closed her door very firmly. I turned to Mr. Potter.

"What are you doing out here?" I hissed at him.

"I was unable to return to sleep after all the noise earlier, so I was going downstairs for a book," he mumbled.

I gestured toward the stairway. "Well, please choose one quickly."

212

His habitual haughty expression returned to his face. "No, thank you. I will just go back to my room."

"Suit yourself."

He slid past the dogs and stumped down the hall. Jack followed him for a few steps until I whispered his name. He turned and came back to Emily Ann and me. I waited until I heard Mr. Potter's door closing, said in a low voice, "Good night, everyone," and led my faithful companions back to Mary Pat's room. Kay slept on, one hand tucked under her cheek, her little snores rising and falling on the chilly air.

22

"I have a little something for you, my dear," Mr. Potter said to me. "I fear I've not been the easiest of guests, and I'd like to make amends. Could you step outside with me for just a moment?"

It was late the next morning, Sunday. I was tired and out of sorts from my interrupted night. I'm embarrassed to admit I had a momentary mental lapse in which I imagined Mr. Potter attempting to ravish me out on the snowy porch of the Bunny Farm Inn. It was so ludicrous that I smiled involuntarily, and since I smiled I felt like I had to agree to go with him. If I smiled and then said no, I might have to explain.

"Sure," I told him. "Just let me grab my jacket." He was already wearing the camel brown top coat in which he had arrived.

I was startled when he brought his left hand out from behind his back holding my jacket. "Voila," he said, proffering it with a stiff little bow. I took it and slipped my arms into the sleeves.

"Let me tell Kay where I'm going," I said, and turned toward the hall.

"Oh, we'll be back in before she even knows you've been out," he assured me, motioning with one of his small hands toward the back door. "I just saw her in the library, she's fine."

I hesitated for a moment, but it was easier to go along with him. I didn't want this to take too long. I would soon need to put cobble together whatever I could find for lunch.

The early morning's thick blanket of snow was now crisscrossed with paths. An enormous snowman loomed in front of the house. I had watched from an upstairs window as Earlene and Doris made snow angels, tall ones and short ones. Kay and Ambrose had trampled out the big circle with spokes needed for a rousing game of Fox and Geese. Kay had gone out "just for a moment" with the dogs after breakfast, and had apparently forgotten her intention of helping me with the dishes. Even Emily Ann had been out there leaping and dashing in the snow.

With everyone except Mr. Potter and Terry playing outside, I was able to straighten their rooms without interference. I made beds, neatened bathrooms, replaced towels, and checked tea-making supplies in all the bedrooms—except Mr. Potter's. I started a load of laundry. I began a batch of bread, and worried over my supply of flour. I looked in on Terry, who still slept.

215

A little while before Mr. Potter showed up in the kitchen, all the snow revelers, including the three dogs, had come laughing into the house. I could hear a shower running in at least one of the upstairs bathrooms as Mr. Potter and I crossed the kitchen. He opened the door for me to pass through onto the back porch. The chill air hit my face. I turned to say something about how cold it was and saw that the Emily Ann, Jack, and Rollo had materialized behind us. "Excuse me," I said to Mr. Potter, and stepped back into the kitchen.

"Wait here," I told the three expectant furry faces. "Stay in the house." I reached down and made sure the locking mechanism was engaged on the large dog door so they couldn't follow me back out into the snow. I thought they'd had enough for one morning. They looked at me reproachfully as Mr. Potter closed the door in their faces. Rollo barked.

"I know this must seem a bit odd," he said, leading the way across the porch and down the steps. I followed carefully as he led the way along one of the paths the company had made through the snow. "But I have something to tell you, and the house is so full of people..."

"True," I agreed, "though since it *is* an inn, I don't suppose that's unexpected."

He kept walking, and I kept following. If I were to be ravished, it wasn't going to be on the porch. After a few more steps I said, "Isn't this is far enough? What did you want to say?"

"Just a little further," he urged, and walked faster. We passed the snow angels, the bench under the

216

arbor, and skirted some twiggy bushes that hid this part of the yard from the house. He stopped then, and turned to face me. "What I have for you is this." He reached into his pocket and pulled something out. It gleamed dark and metallic in the thin winter sunlight.

A gun.

I stared at the thing, then raised my eyes to his face. "You want to give me a gun?" I said in bewilderment. This was even more peculiar than attempted ravishment.

He gave short, sharp shake of his head and snorted. "No, you stupid woman, I really, really want to use it on you." The anger in his voice was stinging.

"What?" I sounded as stupid as he seemed to think I was.

"You ruined everything," he hissed, glaring at me. "I had things under control, my plan was going to work, and then you had to come along. Every time I try to gather my supplies, there you are with those goddam dogs."

People who are pointing guns at you feel they can say anything they want. I'd been here before. It almost made me admire people like Doris who don't need to be armed to speak their minds.

Gun or no, I couldn't make any sense of what Mr. Potter was saying. This guy is a raving lunatic, I told myself, trying to decide what tone of voice would be most soothing. I tried for matter of fact.

"I must be as stupid as you say because I don't have the slightest idea what you are talking about," I said. "All I did was let you stay here, and you didn't even have a reservation."

217

Something flashed into my field of vision. Just as my brain registered that it was Rollo and that he apparently had mastered the small dog door at last, he made a leap for Mr. Potter as he always did. Mr. Potter threw up his hands and stepped back, but the snowy footing proved treacherous. His feet flew out from under him and he went down heavily on his back. The gun flew out of his grasp, gave a little bounce, and landed about two feet away from his out-flung hand.

I know that any self-respecting heroine would have leapt upon the gun and turned the tables on the bad guy. Hell, I'd done it myself back in October with some help from Jack. But my feet were rooted to the ground in horror. The top of Mr. Potter's head had also flown off! Wait, not his head...his hair. A wig. It came to rest near the gun.

Rollo stood on top of Mr. Potter's recumbent body, wriggling with delight and attempting to lick his face. "You goddam repulsive little maw worm," Potter snarled, shoving the dog away and struggling to roll over and reach for the gun. A net covering his real hair fell off. Short curls shook loose. He grabbed the gun, then rolled back over and into a sitting motion, very gracefully for such a tubby man. He reached up to his lip and pulled. The mousy little mustache ripped off.

And then I saw that Mr. Potter was not a tubby man. Mr. Potter was a tubby woman. I finally knew what Rollo had known all along, and done his best to tell everyone.

Mr. Potter was Mary Pat Haskell.

My jaw dropped. No doubt my eyes were bugging out like a cartoon character's. "You—you—" I stammered. My shaking right hand pointed at the figure on the ground.

Rollo returned to Mary Pat, bouncing and wagging. Shoves and epithets discouraged him not at all. She pushed him away again and grabbed the wig and flung it as far as it would go. Wigs are not very aerodynamic, but it flew a few feet, and Rollo chased it. In a moment Mary Pat was on her feet, and the gun was pointed at me again, and we were back where we had started. I hadn't moved an inch. My feet might have frozen to the ground where I stood.

"M-M-M-Mary Pat?" I mewed. "What are you doing?"

Rollo carried the wig to her, growling and shaking it like a rat that needed killing. Mary Pat reached down and jerked it away from Rollo and stuffed it into her pocket, her eyes leaving me for only a brief moment—not long enough to gather my wits and grab the gun.

"I'm leaving," she stated, "and you're going to help me. Follow that path those idiots made to the shed down by the lake." She gestured with the gun. When I hesitated she said, "I'd rather not shoot you here, but I will if I have to. You're a convenience, not a necessity."

I turned my back on her and started along the path she had indicated. Rollo gamboled along between us.

"Faster," she commanded. "I don't want someone to come looking for you too soon."

The contrariness that Miss Irwin had complained of all those years ago in second grade was alive and well and really, really wanted me to walk slower. But gun pointing at your back is powerfully motivating. I picked up my pace.

Maybe if I walked fast enough I could get out of her sight for a moment and somehow turn the tables. But I have yet to find a person over the age of eight who cannot walk faster than me. From the sound of her footsteps thudding on the packed snow, she was keeping pace quite nicely. She even had enough breath to keep talking.

"I swear to god, once I've taken care of you and gotten out of this mess, I'm going to come back here and make sure that flaming Ambrose gets what's coming to him for convincing me to have you come out here."

I felt my chin go up and my back straighten. I will put up with a lot when it's just myself involved, but don't mess with my dogs, and don't diss my friends. Mary Pat didn't know me well enough to recognize the signs, but she had now seriously annoyed me. I don't flare quickly into anger. I have a long fuse. But that fuse had been lit.

"I have no idea what mess you're in, but I came here as a favor," I threw over my shoulder. She muttered something that sounded suspiciously like "Ha!" I still leaned toward the theory that she was simply insane, but an insane person with a gun is no improvement over someone in his right mind.

We followed the twisting path in the snow to a weathered shed that sat about twenty feet from the lakeshore. The padlock was closed, but Mary Pat reached into her pocket and pulled out a ring of keys.

"The key to that lock is the shiny silver one," she said, tossing the keys in my direction. I reached out to catch them but they fell short and I missed. I had to take a step forward and bend down to pick them up. As I straightened with the keys in my hand, I noticed a nasty little smile on her face. Another inch of fuse burned away.

I found the right key and used it. Mary Pat said, "Give me the keys back." I started to toss them to the ground as she had, but she stepped closer and grabbed them from me.

I pushed the shed door open. Inside was a jumble of lawn chairs, a market umbrella, and something dark blue and withered in the corner. Mary Pat pointed to this object.

"Grab that and the paddle and take them down by the lake," she instructed.

Whatever the object was, it was covered with more dirt and cobwebs than I wanted to get involved with. "What is it?" I said, wrinkling my nose.

"It's a canoe," she said, "and you're going to blow it up and row us out of here. Now grab it and get moving. Believe me, I have enough bullets to take care of you and the rest of that pack in the house. If you don't want them all to die, move your ass."

Her gun didn't look big enough to hold bullets for nine people, but I didn't want to put it to the test. Maybe she had more ammunition in her jacket pocket, under the wig that Rollo had tried to kill. I reached down and grabbed the rubber canoe and dragged it toward the door, praying that no spiders would jump on me. This may be the definition of a true phobia, when you're more afraid of a spider than of being shot. The paddle leaned near the door. I tucked it under my arm before pulling the canoe out onto the snow and down to the lake. I spread it out and looked down at it.

"How am I supposed to inflate it? If you want me to blow into it we'll be here for a year. I don't have that much breath in me. Besides, it's filthy," I said. I looked over at her. She was holding a large gym bag in her left hand; she must have picked it up in the shed. She set it down, again without taking her eyes off me.

"There's a foot pump, stupid." She gestured again with the gun. I saw the device she meant and put my foot on it. I gave a push, then another. It hissed a little air into the canoe. "Move it," she demanded. So I started pumping. And pumping and pumping. I changed feet and pumped some more. I don't know why people join expensive health clubs to get exercise when there are devices like this around that you could use in the comfort of your own home. Or lakefront as the case may be.

While I was inflating the canoe, Mary Pat expanded on her earlier statement. "You're lucky I decided just to take you," she informed me. "I did play with the idea of killing everyone in their sleep, getting off the island with the canoe, and coming back as myself when the tragedy was discovered."

"Wouldn't the missing Mr. Potter raise a few questions?" I panted, pumping away.

"What Mr. Potter?" she jeered. "I doubt you told anyone outside the house about his presence, and once I removed his registration information, no one would know there had been another guest. He's going to be awfully hard to find as it is. The authorities will think he was kidnapped and killed too."

I didn't say anything. I had a hard time believing she would really shoot me, but I didn't like that "too."

"Last night was so much fun that I didn't feel like shooting anyone. I really had you going," she went on. Her smug tone set my teeth on edge.

"I didn't think you were enjoying the evening that much," I said. "I didn't see you playing poker with the others."

"Not then, later." She gave an exasperated sigh.

"What, when the dogs caught you going downstairs?"

"I wasn't going downstairs, stupid, I was coming back up." She sniggered.

"What?" I stopped pumping to look at her.

She scowled. "Don't stop. I don't have all day." I started pumping again. "I was coming upstairs from the office. I was there all along."

She *is* nuts, I thought. Next thing she's going to tell me she can walk through walls.

"There's a secret cupboard under the stairs," she went on. "My grandfather built it. He didn't believe in banks and he kept his money there." She nudged the gym bag with her foot. "And I've followed in his footsteps. I only use it for my most valuable stuff."

"What, you've got a whole bag of money there?" I huffed, trying to sound scornful. I was out of breath from my exertions.

Her expression was amused. "Better than that."

I looked away from her and kept pumping until the canoe was taut and three-dimensional. Shaped like a traditional canoe, but shorter and fatter, and with two seats in it. Rollo was intrigued. He began a thorough inspection with his nose.

"All right, get in," Mary Pat said.

I put one foot over the side.

"Oh for god's sake, not here," she snapped. "Put this bag in the center of the boat, push the front half into the water, and get in."

I did as she said. The bag was very heavy. Would it sink the canoe? When the front of the boat was afloat I carefully stepped in, waving my arms to keep my balance as the canoe bobbed on the water.

"Sit in the front seat." I slowly moved forward, trying to figure out how to fold up my legs. I sat awkwardly on the inflated seat. I looked back at Mary Pat, still standing on the shore. She had picked up the paddle and held it out to me. The gun remained steady, so I gave up any thought of somehow using the paddle to attack her and get away. I took the paddle, and faced forward. The canoe rocked as she shoved it further into the water and stepped in.

"All right, paddle," she commanded. "Steer straight for the spit of land that juts out across the way."

I put the paddle in the water and stroked. We barely moved. I have paddled a canoe before, and I was turning the paddle just enough to get very little push. Possibly this was the only useful thing I had learned at summer camp.

"Knock it off and paddle right," she said.

"How? I don't know anything about canoes."

The boat rock again. I looked over my shoulder and saw that Rollo had leapt into the boat with us. He wagged and wiggled toward Mary Pat. She shoved at him with her foot and he tumbled over the bag. "God damn it, you are just a leech with hair!"

I twisted around, grabbed at him with the hand not holding the paddle, and pulled him onto my lap.

"Be careful," I said, "you'll hurt him."

"Dump him out."

"What?"

"Dump him out of this boat," she insisted. "I am not taking that mangy thing with us."

"No," I said. More of the fuse was burning away.

She glared and snarled, "What?"

"No, I won't throw him in the lake," I said.

Her reply to this piece of bravado was to raise the gun. "Do it. Now."

I clutched Rollo to me, and he barked. "You can just go ahead and shoot me right now, Mary Pat Haskell," I said, "but I am not dumping any dog, let alone one this small, into that freezing water. It would kill him, and I will not do it!"

"I'm not going to shoot you," she said, "not yet. I'm going to shoot the dog." She took aim, evidently not considering that any bullet would go through him into me as well.

"No!" I turned away from her and shoved Rollo between my feet. I picked up the oar and began to paddle. The canoe moved away from the shore. She exhaled with a hiss that could have come straight from a cobra.

23

Though the spit of land where we landed the canoe could not be seen from where the bridge had been, it turned out to be a short walk to the inn's parking area. We had to slog through thigh-deep snow to get there—or I did; Mary Pat walked in the path I broke. I tucked Rollo under my arm and carried him, as well as the gym bag that Mary Pat had put into the canoe. Again I noticed its weight.

"What is in here, bricks?" I asked. I couldn't believe it was really full of cash.

"Paper," she replied.

"Paper? It weighs a ton. Why am I toting a ton of paper through the woods?"

"Shut up and walk faster," she demanded. "This is very special paper."

The penny dropped and I stumbled, almost dropping Rollo. "Counterfeiting paper," popped out of my mouth. I peeked over my shoulder at her. She was glaring at me.

"Yes, counterfeiting paper," she said. "Now that I've gotten it out of the house, and removed the computer files, there's only one thing left to tie me to the counterfeit traveler's checks. I don't know where the hell you hid it, but if I couldn't find it probably no one else can either. I'll just stash my supplies somewhere safe and in a few months I can start up again. Keep moving. The parking area is just ahead."

I scowled but didn't say anything else. It seemed a bad sign that she was telling me her plans for future crimes.

Ahead, the parked cars had turned into giant monochrome sculptures in the inn's parking lot. As we stumbled out of the woods I looked across to the island, hoping that someone would be there to see us, but no one was in sight. We had probably not even been missed in the house yet.

I expected Mary Pat to go to her sedan, but instead she headed for the passenger side of Earlene's enormous SUV. "This should do nicely," she said. She slid open the side door. "Put the bag in here and clear the snow off the windows."

I saw Earlene's broom lying on the floor. I set down the bag and the dog and picked it up, hoping I could make a fast turn and surprise her. But she stepped in close beside me and put the gun in my ribs. "Behave yourself," she said.

"Ow," I complained, scowling at her. "Be careful with that thing. I was just getting this to clear off the snow," I said, trying to sound innocent. I wished I knew if the gun was really loaded. I had to assume it was, but it still seemed so unbelievable that someone I knew, someone who liked tea for heaven's sake, was really holding me at gunpoint.

She followed me as I swept snow off the SUV, then back to the side door. "All right, get in the driver's seat."

I climbed into the SUV. I couldn't get into the driver's seat without removing Earlene's cushion, so I tossed it onto the floor in front of the passenger seat. Rollo followed me into the car and jumped onto the passenger seat, looking ready to go anywhere. His breath hung white in the car's frigid air as he panted happily.

As I climbed into the front, Mary Pat stepped up into the car and slid the door shut.

I could still barely get behind the steering wheel because the seat was pushed so far forward. "I have to slide the seat back," I said, and gave it a shove. When I looked back at Mary Pat I saw that she settled herself onto the bench seat behind me and was holding the ring of keys out to me.

"All right," she said, "find the right key and let's get going."

My seat was now so far back I had to lean forward to see out of the side window and I felt like I could barely reach the steering wheel, even though it was roughly as big around as a hula hoop. But Earlene's foot extenders on the pedals still bent my knees awkwardly. I fastened my seat belt and looked at the ring of keys. Besides the shiny silver one I had used to open the shed, there were three or four that looked like car keys, and some that probably opened the doors to the inn, and one long, old fashioned one. I found the key with the insignia for the make of Earlene's car, put it in the ignition and turned it, hoping that the cold weather would make the SUV refuse to start. It fired right up. I released the parking brake, put the transmission into drive, and hoped the deep snow would keep us from moving. The four-wheel whale moved forward smoothly as soon as I touched the gas. I accelerated a bit, thinking I might be able to hit the brakes to force a slide and dislodge Mary Pat, but then I heard her seatbelt click behind me. I sighed and crept down the lane.

"How did you get Earlene's keys?" I asked.

"I only took the car key," Mary Pat replied. "She left them on the kitchen table while she was upstairs cleaning my room. I knew she wouldn't miss just one key."

The cleared area through the trees was my only hint of where to drive, but the SUV didn't care if it was on a road or not. As we crawled down the lane, I said, "Did you know Earlene had a big car, or did you take everyone's car key just in case? What if Earlene had a car like Miss Mason and Miss Gray, for instance?"

She gave a derisive snort just as I neared the end of the lane. "Turn left. And for your information, those two women are not Miss Mason and Miss Gray."

"What?" In my surprise my foot stepped harder on the brake than I had intended and the SUV fishtailed before stopping. Mary Pat gave an inarticulate snarl. I rocked forward, as I had so many times in this car, and the seatbelt tightened just before I hit the steering wheel. As I rocked back some information registered in my brain: Something hard was lodged between the belt and my ribs. Something in my inside coat pocket.

"They are not Miss Mason and Miss Gray," she repeated. "I don't know who they are, probably cops of some kind, but they are not the schoolteachers from High Cross who own this stupid dog."

I looked at Rollo before I turned back to check the road. No wonder he ignored his owners—they weren't his owners. They must have borrowed him for the weekend. I wondered who they really were, and if the fact that they were not schoolteachers from High Cross might mean they would notice we were not in the house and come and rescue Rollo and me.

Probably not.

At the same time, I was feverishly trying to think what the hell was in my pocket. Dog toy? Dog treats? Glasses case?

The county highway was completely covered with snow, but I saw the tracks of at least a couple of cars. It must be passable. I started to turn right.

"Left!" Mary Pat shouted at me, startling me so that I stamped on the gas as I jerked the steering wheel. The back end of the SUV flew around in a faster arc than the front. I managed to straighten the car and continued in the direction Mary Pat intended to go.

"Don't yell at me like that," I protested, feeling another inch or two of fuse burn away.

That's when I remembered.

I had the missing cell phone from the Bunny Farm Inn in my pocket. I had turned it off while I was buying groceries, and stuck it in there so I wouldn't lose it. And I hadn't. All I had done was forget where it was, but this phone certainly wasn't lost.

"I'll do more than yell at you if you try anything like that again," Mary Pat promised. She reached forward and poked me hard with the gun barrel, and I flinched away.

I wanted to reach over the seat and smack her.

I drove carefully along the county road. "Where are we going?" I asked, hoping we'd be passing some population center where I might be able to attract some attention.

"Not far," she said. "About a mile, then you'll turn right beside an old mailbox." I could hear a hint of satisfaction in her voice.

I was sure I knew the place—the house Earlene and I had looked at yesterday morning. The one that had a long, old fashioned key like the one on the ring swinging from the SUV's ignition. The house I didn't want to buy, the house that probably no one would want to buy. The house without any close neighbors, that no one would come near for who knows how long.

The house that would be a dandy place to kill someone and leave her body while you got away with murder.

Suddenly it was hard to force the cold air in and out of my lungs.

I sped up, hoping I could miss the turn into the driveway when it came, just to buy some time. It didn't work.

"Slow down," she commanded. "Before we get to the turnoff, I want to know what the hell you did with the porcelain figurine from your cousin's store?"

"Figurine?" Since she had told me to slow down, I took my foot off the accelerator. Maybe if I drifted to a stop someone would come along. I looked hopefully in the rear view mirror but there were no cars in sight. There was, however, something moving along the road, a low dark shape. I squinted. Was it a deer? The shape seemed wrong.

"You know what I'm talking about. The porcelain figurine that was hidden in the bookcase. I need it back."

Should I tell her? "It's in a safe place," I said. "Let me go and I'll give it to you."

"I don't need it that badly," she assured me. "No one knows that house like I do. When I can search it properly, I'll find the damned thing."

"Why do you want it? Does the woman you got it from want it back or something?" I asked. We were slowing to a crawl. Ahead was the overpass that Earlene and I had slid on yesterday. Maybe I could do that again, even slide off into the creek. It probably wasn't all that deep. I glanced again into the side mirror. Whatever was coming down the road was a little closer. I moved my head slightly so I could see Mary Pat in the mirror. She was watching me and not looking outside.

"You mean your cousin? I expect she does."

"No, I mean the woman with the eyebrows who came into the store and bought it with the fake

232

traveler's checks. Is she a relative of yours? Kay thought it was a family doing it."

I was startled when Mary Pat began to laugh. "You ninny," she said, "you still don't get it, do you? They were all me."

"What? That was you with the eyebrows?"

Her voice took on a note of exasperation. "Of course it was me, they were all me. The teenage girl and the old woman and the middle aged man and all the rest of them."

"No!" I said, then caught her expression in the mirror. "I mean, wow. That's amazing."

"No one looks at you if you're not thin and beautiful. You know that. I wanted to act more than I wanted to breathe, but no one will cast a frumpy woman as anything other than someone's mother or aunt. I ended up with that stupid inn serving breakfast to losers who don't know any better than to take a vacation in Willow County. With their dogs, no less." Her contempt was palpable.

"But couldn't you have sold the inn?"

"I tried. But then I saw what a great cover it was. I've been passing this paper all over the world for ages. Every year on that stupid bed and breakfast tour, I'd use it in whatever country we traveled to."

"You must have enough money to go anywhere. Just ditch the tours."

"I did, of course." Duh, said her tone. "I started passing my checks in Atlantic City, then Reno and Las Vegas. Okay, I overdid it this time in Vegas. My luck is usually good, but this time I was running short. I passed more of my checks, and they were already looking for them. They don't mess around in those casinos." An aggrieved note crept into her voice. "It's okay for them to take the customers' money, but they really resent it when someone turns the tables on them. But I got away, and I'll get away from here too. That figurine is the only local thing I bought that can be tied to the counterfeits. But it doesn't matter if you tell me. I'm sure you told your cousin where it is."

"No," I said. "I didn't tell anyone. I never had a chance. We haven't had a minute alone except last night and one or the other of us was asleep the whole time."

"Yeah, right," she scoffed. "I bet. Anyway, all I have to do is come back as someone Kay has never seen before and I won't have any trouble making her tell me where the damned figurine is."

"I tell you she doesn't know," I insisted. "I'll give you the blasted thing. It was my mother's and Kay was selling it for me. You can have it, and that will be the end of it."

She snorted. "Well, it might be if you also gave me eight hundred thousand dollars. That would be about enough to buy off the mafia guys running the casinos I scammed."

"Eight—" I choked, and stopped. No wonder she was on the run. And that was the moment I realized I had not believed that she would really shoot me.

Until now.

24

The van had slowed to a crawl while she talked, and we had crossed the creek without my noticing it. We were almost to the turnoff. I pushed down too hard on the accelerator and the SUV began to fishtail.

"Enough of that," she said. "Turn right by that mailbox and drive up to the house."

Oh, god, I thought, she really is going to take me in there and shoot me. The chill air in the car was nothing compared to the coldness I felt inside. I had a cell phone in my pocket that I didn't see how I could possibly use before she took it away or killed me. All it did was give me a glimmer of hope that I had no way of redeeming.

I looked in the big side mirror one more time as I automatically pushed up the turn signal. Finally I could make out the dark object moving on the road. His furry body stayed low to the ground and his head jutted forward as he rushed toward us.

Jack.

Would a cell phone in my pocket and Jack be enough to save me?

The driveway to the abandoned house had disappeared under the snow. If I had not been here the previous day, I would never have believed a drive existed. I suddenly wondered if she knew that I had been here the day before. If not, what advantage might that give me? Had she purloined the key from Earlene, or did she have one of her own?

"What do you mean, turn right?" I protested. "We'll get stuck in a field." I tried to look as though I were studying the terrain.

"Damn it, turn when I say turn!" she snarled. "There's a driveway beside that mailbox."

I stopped the SUV in the road a few feet before the mailbox in question. "But I can't see anything," I said. "How can I drive off the road if I have no idea where I'm going? I could wreck us."

I heard her draw her breath in, and a moment later I felt the cold ring of the gun barrel press against my neck.

"If I have to shoot you through the throat," she whispered right behind my head, "you probably won't die right away."

I have read about fear making your blood turn to ice in your veins. Take it from me, it's incredibly uncomfortable.

I took my foot off the brake, pressed the gas pedal gently, and turned right just before the rusted mailbox. When she eased the gun away from my skin I let out my breath. The surge of relief fanned new life into the glowing fuse of my anger.

The tops of the fence posts were still visible, each sporting a jaunty top hat of white. I followed their line and plowed my way through the powder. The curve to the left, then the right, then the hill—I felt the wheels start to slip. I let it roll back some, hoping Mary Pat would think the rise too great to climb in the snow.

"Put this sucker in low gear and drive," she said. I put it in low gear and drove, slowly, slowly. We slipped a bit and fishtailed as we reached the top of the rise, and then we were in front of the house. I glanced in the side mirror again.

Jack had almost caught up with the SUV.

"Climb back here and open the side door and get out," Mary Pat said. "Move slowly and don't try anything stupid. I'll be right behind you."

I swiveled in my seat and wriggled into the back, bending my head so I wouldn't hit the ceiling. As I reached for the door release, Rollo jumped out of the passenger seat and bounced beside me, eager to be out in the snow again. I unlatched the door and as I began to pull it open, I reached over with my little finger and hit the lock button. When the door was open a couple of feet Rollo jumped down. I followed him and turned, my hand on the outside handle.

Mary Pat started to climb out of the car. Her attention was on me, not the ground, and she was taken by surprise when Jack ran up to the open door and jumped at her. She flinched back into the interior of the SUV, Jack dropped to the ground, and I rammed the door shut. As I did, her gun went off with a reverberating crack. Fortunately it was pointing up, and only blasted a hole in the top of Earlene's car. I turned and ran as fast as I could through the thigh deep snow toward the house, both dogs barreling behind me. The deep snow slowed my steps, but Mary Pat had to be deafened and hopefully confused by the gun going off.

At least I had the answer to the question about it being loaded or not, though it was not the answer I was hoping for.

I didn't hear the car door slide open by the time I reached the porch. With shaking hands I managed to get the big old-fashioned key into the lock and gave it a quarter turn to the right. The dogs and I tumbled into the house. I pulled the key out of the lock, slammed the door shut and twisted the brass knob over the keyhole. The lock snicked shut again. Through the glass in the door I saw Mary Pat struggling to get the car door open. She must finally have connected with the lock mechanism. The door began to slide.

Rollo and Jack both shook themselves hard, and I kicked off my boots in the front hall so that I wouldn't leave a trail of snow. We dashed up the stairs, into the front bedroom with the fireplace. I tugged at the cabinet door. It was stuck. I tugged harder, muttering over and over, "Open, damn it, open, damn it." The incantation finally worked. The door flew open, nearly dumping me on the floor. I grabbed Rollo, called, "Jack, here!" and leapt into the hidden space beside the chimney. I heard glass shatter downstairs. Mary Pat must be in the house. I pulled the door shut.

In the confined space, Jack pressed against my legs, and I could feel him panting hard. Almost as hard as I was myself. I tucked Rollo under my right arm while I reached into the left side of my jacket and pulled the cell phone out of the inside pocket. Its tiny dial lit up when I flipped it open, illuminating the cobwebs hanging down in my face. With a shaking finger I dialed 911.

The call connected and rang, then rang again. A third ring. Then a woman's voice said, "Emergency services, what is the nature of your emergency?"

"Oh, please," I whispered as loud as I dared, "Mary Pat has a gun and she's going to kill me!"

A tiny silence, then professional calm. "You are with someone who is threatening to shoot you? Where are you, ma'am?"

My hand was shaking so hard I could barely hold the phone. "I—I'm in an abandoned house on the county road on the east side of the lake—"

Under my arm, Rollo began to writhe, and Jack vibrated with a low growl. And then the door to the hidden space swung open, and there was Mary Pat with the gun in her hand. She stepped in close and put the gun to my head.

"Hang up," she hissed. A rattlesnake could have been no more venomous. I pushed the button to stop the call. She moved back. Grabbing my sleeve, she pulled me out of the cupboard, swinging me around so my back was to the window. She stood in the open doorway of the hiding place I had thought was so secret. I dropped Rollo and he rolled halfway across the room on the bare boards until he could scramble to his feet. Jack was still in the space behind Mary Pat, watching me intently.

239

The winter light from the windows behind me fell on Mary Pat's face. I saw she had lost one of her blue contact lenses. Somehow the mismatched eyes were even more disconcerting than the single unwinking stare of the gun barrel.

"Thought you'd gotten away, didn't you?" she spat at me. "I grew up a mile from this place. Did you really think I wouldn't know about this place? I used to play with the kids who lived here. Where do you think my grandfather got the idea for his hidden room?"

"Mary Pat," I said, somehow not wanting to sound as desperate as I felt, "you really do not want to escalate to murder. All you've done so far is print up some money that wasn't real. I don't care about the figurine you got from Kay's store. I would have given you the damned thing. I never liked it. I wish I'd broken it when I was eight instead of just chipping it. But if you shoot me they'll find you and—"

The cell phone I still held in my hand began to ring.

I don't know which of us was more startled. She reached for the phone to grab it as I managed to connect with the answer button.

"Louisa? Is that you? I've been trying to reach you for ages." It was Bob's voice. He sounded normal and cheerful and very, very far away.

I caught back a sob on its way out "Oh, hi, Ed," I said. "How are you?"

Mary Pat lunged for the phone with an outstretched hand. I twisted to avoid her.

"No, it's Bob," he said, his voice puzzled.

"That's right, Ed," I said. "Earlene and I did look at that house." Maybe Bob, out there in San Francisco, would be disturbed enough to call Ed and somehow Ed would come and save me.

In the next few seconds.

Didn't seem likely.

"Louisa, are you all right?" Worry sharpened his voice.

Mary Pat grabbed my arm and shoved the gun against my ribs.

"Um, no, Ed. Listen, this isn't a good time. I—I have to go."

I disconnected the call. She reached with her left hand for the phone. I flinched back and the phone fell from my shaking hand. Rollo dashed across the room and began to bark at it.

Mary Pat choked out, "God damn dog!" She pulled the gun away from my ribs and turned, aiming the gun at him. As though my glasses were telephoto lenses, I zoomed in as her finger tightened on the trigger.

"No!" I cried, and almost involuntarily flailed out my arms, making contact with the hand that held the gun.

It went off, flames spurting mere inches from my shoulder. I shrieked. Jack yelped. Rollo barked. I twisted and gave Mary Pat a shove.

The force of my push knocked her backward into Jack, who still stood behind her. She tried to keep her balance by waving her arms wildly in the air, the gun windmilling in a crazed circle before she upended over the dog into the space beside the fireplace. Jack yelped

241

again and scrambled toward me. I slammed the cupboard door shut on Mary Pat. I put my back against it, bracing my stockinged feet on the floor, but my knees had lost their gel and I slid into a sitting position. My limp weight on the lower part of the door was enough to keep her from shoving it back open.

There are times it pays not to be anorexic.

"God damn it, let me out of here!" came her muffled voice. I felt the door shake. She must be throwing herself against it. Jack bustled up and began kissing my face.

"Oh, Jack," I told him, "you and Rollo came through."

An explosion resounded over my head. Plaster rained down on us. The window opposite crashed into shards. My peripheral vision darkened as I visualized what would have happened if I hadn't slid to the floor.

And the long fuse on my anger burned away completely.

I shoved myself back to my feet. The door juddered against my back. She had reverted to trying to push her way out. Another thud, then another. I had the rhythm now, and jerked with all my might as she threw herself against the door one more time.

She catapulted out of the secret room, fell over Jack yet again, and crashed to the floor. The gun flew out of her hand and slid several feet away. Rollo chased it, barking. I scrambled to sit down on Mary Pat. The air in her lungs went out in a loud "Oof!"

"Ha!" Glee filled my heart. I gave a little bounce of triumph. I felt like I'd invented a new form of martial arts, where sitting on one's opponent was the highest goal.

"Ow!" she whined, beating at my leg with a fist."Get off, you're crushing me. I can't hear, my ears have gone numb. Let me go!"

At the sound of her voice, Rollo abandoned the gun and came running to lick her face. She turned her face the other direction, only to find Jack there, baring his shining white teeth. I felt the fight go out of her. At the same moment, Rollo whirled to face the door and began to bark once more. Running footsteps in the hall, and then the doorway was filled by an imposing figure, his unwavering gun held out by two straight arms.

Ed.

I gaped at him in amazement. "What—how—"

"Louisa! Are you okay?" He lowered his gun and stepped into the room. "Do you need help?"

I shook my head and took a deep, grateful breath. "I did a few minutes ago, but everything's just fine now."

25

The sign on the door of the Bluebird Cafe read:

Private party
By invitation only
Come back tomorrow!

Inside, all the tables had been pushed together in the center of the room to seat everyone. Dorothy, the Bluebird's chef, had outdone herself in the kitchen; I didn't think I'd ever been so well fed. Now she and Cleta had cleared the tables and drawn their own chairs close. Champagne corks had popped, and the bubbly wine had been poured into a set of delicate crystal flutes Kay had brought over from the store. A clear note like the song of a lark rang out whenever anyone tapped one.

Bob's chair was pulled close beside mine. A warm strip crossed my back where his arm lay along the top of my chair. He raised his wine glass and said in a carrying voice, "May I propose a toast?"

The voices that had been talking and laughing around the table quieted.

"I'd like to drink a toast to my dog Jack," Bob went on. "His legs are short, but his courage and stamina are long. To Jack!"

Jack was sitting on the other side of Bob, on a wide chair. He wore a souvenir bandana printed with scenes of San Francisco that Bob had brought home for him. On his head he sported a sparkly party hat. He thumped his tail when he heard his name, and we drank his toast.

Nearly two weeks had passed since that ill-fated Sunday when Mr. Potter invited me outside. I'd heard most of the stories of that day—some several times.

As Mary Pat had hoped, it took a while for anyone to notice my absence. What had not gone into Mary Pat's equation was the dogs.

Dogs can hear four times as well as people; a sound that I could hear a block away, they can hear four blocks away. Emily Ann and Jack could hear our conversation in the back yard of the inn. They would have recognized the shock in my voice when Mr. Potter turned into Mary Pat. That may have been when they headed to the kitchen to go out the dog door. But the big dog door had been locked, and Jack could only get his head through the small one, which he did.

Emily Ann sought out Kay and William, who were in the library comparing travel experiences. Kay petted Emily Ann absently and told her to go lie down, but my usually obedient greyhound had stood resolutely looking into Kay's face. So Kay said, "Emily Ann, go to Louisa," and Emily Ann went out of the room to try the dog door again. Jack had not been able to unlock it and still had his head through the small door. Emily Ann went back to the library and put her head in Kay's lap.

Kay broke off her conversation. "Emily Ann, what is the matter with you? Can't you find Louisa?"

I'm sure Emily Ann replied that I was not in the house, but other people do not understand your dog as well as you do.

Kay looked at William. "I wonder if Louisa forgot to feed the dogs this morning."

"Maybe she just needs to go out. Do you want me to take her?" he offered.

"That's all right, I can go," she said. She looked at Emily Ann and said, "Is that it? Do you want to go out?"

The O word was the one Emily Ann was waiting to hear, and she perked up her ears, whipped her tail back and forth, and headed for the back door. Kay and William followed. But before they got to the kitchen, Ambrose called to Kay from Terry's room. She veered off to see what he wanted.

"Kay," Ambrose said, "have you seen Louisa?"

"Not since breakfast," she said. "Do you know if Louisa fed the dogs this morning?"

"She did," he told her. "I was in the kitchen when they were crunching away. She had me lock the dog door so they couldn't leave without her and get lost in the snow."

"Maybe that's why Emily Ann seems desperate to go out," she said. "I'll be back in a few minutes."

Kay and William went to the kitchen. where they saw Jack with his head stuck through the small dog door.

"Uh-oh," said Kay. "I bet Rollo got out. He must finally have figured out how to push through. Maybe that's what Emily Ann's been trying to tell us." She grabbed her coat from the rack by the door and slid her arms into the sleeves. "Don't you need a coat?" she asked William.

"Nope, this sweater is wool. I'll just borrow this muffler," he said, pulling one off the rack and flinging it around his neck. "I don't feel the cold much."

Kay turned to Jack and poked his butt. "Hey, Jack, you're going to have to move so we can go out."

Again the O word worked its magic. Jack backed out of the small dog door, and he and Emily Ann waited tensely for Kay to let them out. As soon as she did, they were off running.

"Oh dear," said Kay, "they may be after a rabbit. We'd better follow them. If they fall in a hole Louisa will never forgive me."

The deep snow slowed the dogs and made their trail easy to follow. Their tracks headed straight for the bridge landing.

William and Kay followed as quickly as they could. When they reached the spot where the bridge should have been, Emily Ann was pacing back and forth along the shore, whining, and Jack was swimming toward the parking lot.

"Jack! Come back!" Kay called, but William put out a hand and gripped her arm so hard that she found bruises later.

"Kay, look," he said, pointing with his other hand. Kay raised her eyes from the black dog swimming steadily through the icy water.

"What the hell!" she cried. "Someone is stealing Earlene's car!"

"Not someone," William said. "That's Louisa in the driver's seat."

Jack reached the other side, climbed out of the water, and gave a tremendous shake that sent water in all directions. Then he took off after the SUV that had trundled out of sight around a bend.

Now, at the café, Emily Ann sat between Kay and me at the banquet table. Emily Ann was so tall that she didn't need a chair, but she had been provided with a large cushion. Kay handed her one of the home-made dog biscuits that the Bluebird serves to their four-legged customers. "She needs to toast Jack too," Kay said to me.

"Well, let me have one for Jack," I said. "Can't leave the honoree out." Kay handed me another treat, which I handed to Bob, who balanced it on Jack's nose for a moment before saying, "Okay!" The morsel instantly disappeared behind Jack's large white teeth.

"I have a toast too," Ed said. "To Earlene's sister Gina. If Gina were not the woman she is, I wouldn't have been out trying to get to the inn to find out what had happened to Earlene. The timing was a gift from the gods, but sometimes the gods need a little help."

Everyone raised their glasses toward the two sisters, sitting side by side across the table from me. They had the same curved nose and lustrous dark hair, but Gina was nearly a foot taller than Earlene. You knew they were sisters, though, because they talked just alike.

"Well, I was worried," Gina said when we drank the toast. "Earlene may drive like a maniac and go careering around the county showing houses any time of the day or night but she's always been reliable and it wasn't like her to not come home. She was supposed to go with me to my scrapbooking class that evening and I waited so long for her to show up that I missed the class, because Edna Bingham who teaches will not let you come in late. I just hope I get to graduate from the class, because she doesn't let you miss any either. Though I did hear through the grapevine that the class was called off because of the snow, and Edna better not try to make out differently.

"So, with all that snow I was afraid something had happened to Earlene. I knew she was showing Louisa some house at the lake and I figured she'd gotten snowed in out there, hopefully at the inn and not in some empty house. But I had a bad dream that night and I don't remember what happened in it but when I got up I said to Danny Joe that we had to go out to the Bunny Farm and get Earlene, and he said he wasn't driving anywhere in this snow and I belonged at the Funny Farm Inn if I thought he was. Well, ha, ha, ha, I said, thank you very much, a fat lot of help you are. And I was going to just get in the pickup and go by myself but then, just as clear as if someone was

249

standing beside me, a voice said to me, Gina, call Ed, because Kay was supposed to be out there too and I could find out whether he had heard from her."

Evidently the town did not take Kay and Ed's off-again periods too seriously. The fact that someone I had never met knew where my cousin was supposed to be was business as usual in Willow Falls.

"So I did," Gina went on, "I called and got that Kerry Sue Maddock on the phone, and I'm sorry to have to say this, Ed, but you have got the stupidest woman in Willow Falls answering your phone for you."

Kay reached over Emily Ann to poke me; she has often said the same thing about Kerry Sue. But Gina didn't pause.

"All she had to do was tell me whether you were at the police station or not but no, she had to be all mysterious and why was I calling and she would see that you got the message. I said to myself, nuh-uh, Kerry Sue, I wouldn't trust you to tie a shoe for a two year old, let alone give someone a message. So I just hung up on Miss Kerry Sue and called Ed's house and got his mama on the phone. And *she* told me that Ed was still asleep, he'd been on duty late the night before, but I said I was worried about my sister Earlene and I wanted Ed to come with me out to the lake.

"Well, Earlene had helped Ed buy that house they live in, and his mama always liked it that Earlene got my boys to help them move in, so she went and got Ed out of bed and told him to pick me up and go find Earlene. So he did."

"She poked me and gave me a piece of toast with peanut butter on it and told me to drive carefully, and off I went with this crazy woman who thought something was wrong because she'd had a bad dream." Ed shook his head. "But you know my mother—"

This time it was my turn to nudge Kay.

"—so I drove carefully out to the lake. We came around the last bend before the turnoff to the Bunny Farm to see this SUV about to disappear over the next rise on the county road. And Gina said—"

"I said, hey, that's my sister's car," Gina jumped back in, "and Ed said there are lots of cars like that on the road and it could be anyone's, and he tried to turn—"

"She didn't like that." Ed grinned at Gina from his place beside Kay. "I thought I had a live wildcat in the car. So I stayed on the road—"

"You just about had us in the ditch, sliding around," Gina grinned back.

"What do you expect when you grab someone's steering wheel on a snowy road like that?" Ed retorted. "Anyway, I kept going the direction the SUV had gone. You know how the road dips and rises along there. We kept catching sight of the car and then it would disappear again."

"And I said, there's something following along behind them," Gina said, "but we were still too far back to see that it was Jack, and we couldn't speed up because of the snow. So when we got to the place where Louisa had turned off they were already out of sight, but I saw the tire tracks in the snow and I remembered that the house Earlene was going to show

251

Louisa wasn't very far from the inn, so I made Ed turn in and follow those tracks. He said they could have been made by anybody but I just knew they were the right ones, and when we got up by the house, there was her car all right, with a big old hole blasted in the top of it.

"Well, Ed changed into a cop right before my eyes. It was just amazing. One minute I'm in this old four-wheel drive thing with a regular guy and two seconds later I'm sitting next to the Terminator. He was out of that car and up to the house like an eel, and I watched him ease that front door open and listen and damn if he didn't have a gun out and everything. That's about when I opened my car door. I heard a dog bark, and Ed disappeared into the house. Well, I couldn't sit there by myself not knowing what was going on. If my sister was in there I decided I was going in there too, so I got out and tried to sneak up like Ed did only I'm not a cop and all I did was trip on a stick that was hidden under the snow. Fell right on my face. Then I heard a gunshot.

"By the time I got back on my feet and started for the house again, here comes Ed holding onto this woman in handcuffs. She was cussing up a blue storm and trying to kick Ed in the knee. Lord, that woman has a mouth on her. He marched her over to his four wheeler and got her into the back seat and managed to undo one of the cuffs and shut it back on a handle bolted to the wall, and then he turned around and there was Louisa stumbling out of the house with the two dogs and he walked back over and gave her the biggest old hug and she and I had never met but we took one look at each other and we both started crying. I had no idea what we were crying for but if she was going to cry I figured somebody ought to cry with her."

Gina looked across the table at me. When Ed let go of me that Sunday she had stepped up and wrapped her arms around me and said, "There you go, honey, you're okay now." I felt like she was channeling Kay, who was still prowling up and down the lakeshore trying to think of some way to get off the island so she could save me, wherever I was, while everyone else scoured the island looking for traces of me and Mr. Potter.

Sisters, cousins.

We smiled at each other.

Terry sat on the far side of Earlene, his wine glass filled with ginger ale.

"I have a toast too," he piped up. We looked at him expectantly. "For Miss Mason and Miss Gray. Only, like, they aren't really Miss Mason and Miss Gray? Because I got an A on my social studies paper from Mr. Pearlman and I never thought that would happen in a million years and it was all because of them?" He raised his glass in their direction, and we all drank another sip.

"He just gave you that A because we showed up in his classroom armed," teased the woman we had known as Miss Mason. She and the erstwhile Miss Gray were seated near the end of the table across from me, next to two other ladies.

"We owe a big debt to the real Miss Mason and Miss Gray," she went on, smiling at the women beside her. "Lending us Rollo and their reservation at the Bunny Farm Inn was above and beyond, as they say."

Secret Service Agents Nina Alexander and Cordelia Simmons' investigation into the counterfeit traveler's checks had led them to Mary Pat Haskell as a prime suspect. They knew that Mary Pat was traveling and that someone else would be minding the inn.

"We figured we would be on the spot when Mary Pat returned," Agent Simmons said. "And if we just happened to find any evidence in the house—"

"Like that supply of paper she hauled out along with you," Agent Alexander said to me.

"Or some files on the computer?" I asked.

Agent Simmons nodded. "Exactly. And of course there was always the possibility you were an accomplice. When you disappeared at the same time she did, well, I had two pairs of handcuffs warmed up and ready to go."

Kay hitched herself up in her chair, scowling. "Louisa would never—"

Nina Alexander chuckled. "We know that now. And of course you were one of the victims of the counterfeit travelers checks, and it was unlikely that Louisa would be involved in robbing you. But we had to consider all the possibilities. Unfortunately, we did not consider the possibility that Mr. Potter was Mary Pat."

"And naturally he—she—darn, this is so confusing!" her partner said. "Naturally Mary Pat knew we were not Rollo's real owners."

"You should have, like, listened to the dog," Terry put in.

"Mary Pat did tell me the Rollo was crazy about her," I said. "His taste in people is, um, eccentric."

The real Misses Mason and Gray laughed out loud.

"I really appreciated your help with Mr. Pearlman," Terry said to the agents. "Coming to my class was, like, huge? And it even got my mom off my back."

Even in his measled state, Terry had been quick to recognize a unique opportunity when it was revealed who had been posing as Rollo's owners. He interviewed them from his sick bed, and as soon as he could sit up long enough, he wrote an excellent paper on counterfeiting and the role of the Secret Service in its control. Given the circumstances, Mr. Pearlman agreed to accept the paper a week late.

"Our pleasure," said Agent Simmons. "Though if the old man had stopped lecturing us on the history of the Secret Service it might have been a more interesting hour!"

"Duh," muttered Terry.

"Amen," muttered Kay.

Agent Alexander held up a hand. "As you may have heard, Mary Pat was denied bail, since we are certain she would disappear instantly. But we learned just today that she is in the infirmary—with the measles."

Everyone applauded and cheered. We raised our glasses to Terry.

"We have another toast," she went on. "William, even though it brought Mary Pat back to the inn days before we expected her, we have to thank you for the series of articles you wrote in Las Vegas on the counterfeiting. She was already getting nervous, and you shocked her into running back home to grab her supplies. With her talent for becoming other people, if she had decided to disappear straight from Las Vegas, we might never have found her."

"You weren't the only ones to figure out Mary Pat was a suspect," William said. William Jones, it turned out, was only part of his name. He was more often known as W. J. Conover, an investigative reporter for the Chicago *Tribune*, and the author of the syndicated article that we had read in the High Cross paper about counterfeiters in Las Vegas. "When I got a couple of casino owners to talk off the record about what they would do to the counterfeiter when they found her, it scared me half to death. I can only imagine how Mary Pat must have felt. It's no wonder she ran.

"Besides," he went on, "going to the inn for the weekend seemed like a good opportunity to combine business with pleasure." He reached over and squeezed Doris's hand. She tilted her head and gave him a taunting look.

"And was I the business part, or the pleasure?" she asked.

"Oh, pleasure," he assured her. "Pure, pure pleasure, Dorrie honey."

Earlene bounced to the edge of her chair. "Well, before you two start to bill and coo like newlyweds, I get to have my turn. After all, I did make the bed and clean the bathroom for the grouchiest person I have ever had the misfortune to meet. Who, besides being grouchy, was making funny money and nearly killed my friend Louisa, and if that's not bad enough also shot out the top of my car and ruined it so I had to go buy another and you know the insurance company never gives you enough when something like that happens." She paused to draw breath, and looked over at me and Bob. "I want to make a toast to Louisa's honey Bob, who has the best old black dog in the world, and he also went all the way to San Francisco and found a house for Louisa while he was there that she just purely loves, and they let me make the deal and we signed the papers today. Bob, I don't know what I'll do with my time now that I won't be driving Louisa around, but I raise my glass to anyone who could find that woman a house!"

I leaned over and kissed Bob's cheek before drinking another sip of my wine. Because he had indeed found my new home.

"Imagine talking to another hypnotist at brunch," Bob told the group, "and finding out she was from Willow Falls. Not only that, her dad passed away a few weeks ago, and she needed to sell her parents' house. If humans had ears like dogs', mine would have been standing up like a collie's." He reached over to Jack and fondled one of his droopy ears.

"The more she told me about it, the more excited I got," he went on. "So I called Louisa on the off chance she might answer the phone." I poked him in the ribs. "Which she did, but then she kept calling me Ed and I knew from her voice something was terribly wrong." He looked at me. "I may never let you out of my sight again."

I gave an involuntary shiver, remembering. "I know, I was so scared when I turned that phone off, but at least you had lent me Jack."

When Bob had returned from San Francisco, we went with Earlene to see the house. It was on the edge of town, on a winding, tree-lined lane that climbed up from the river. The driveway rose away from the street and curved around a small hill, then ended in a clearing by a detached garage. The house was built into the hillside, nestled among a grove of large trees with bark that reminded me of my summer camp refuge. I suspected that when the trees leafed out in spring I would recognize the shape of the new leaves.

When I saw the house, my heart quickened. It was round, or actually octagonal, with walls of floor-to-ceiling glass. The entry was on the lower side of the hill, sheltered by a deck above. Inside, a circular stairway emerged into a large space utterly filled with light. The ceiling was high, and the space was undivided except for a wedge on the north side for a bedroom and bath. I could see where my dining table would fit near the kitchen, and the cobalt blue wood-stove would be the center of a conversation area. I turned, taking in all the light, and saw that several of the windows were actually French doors opening onto a deck that curved around several sides of the house. The deck jutted out into the trees.

I'd found a tree house for grownups.

I turned around and Bob read my expression.

"Earlene, it's time for Louisa to buy a house," he said, and they high-fived each other.

I had nodded. "It's not a silo or a cave, but let's do it!"

I pulled myself back from thoughts of my new home to the happy group packed into the Bluebird Cafe. A cheerful buzz arose as those who had seen my new place described it to the ones who hadn't.

Gina waved her hand in the air for attention. "Did you all hear what happened to Earlene when she went to that real estate broker's meeting the other day?" Around the table people shook their heads. "They gave her a special award, all done up in a beautiful oak frame, for showing the most properties to a single person in one county. Apparently she and Louisa set some kind of record."

I shook my head. "Well, you're safe from getting another one. I never plan to move again."

The group laughed, then a voice rose above the rest and silenced us all.

"Lew-eeeee-sa!" Doris, of course. "How did I end up last in line? I meant to go first and all of you keep cutting ahead of me." She looked around the table, gathering her audience in. "I propose a toast to the woman who has brought us all to this table tonight. I have known Louisa McGuire for many years, though not as well as I should have. I knew that she was kind and hard-working and loyal. Actually she takes the loyalty thing *way* beyond reason." She stopped to roll her eyes. Doris will always be Doris. "To this list I now add that she's one of the bravest people I have ever met, and she makes a damn fine pot of tea. To Louisa!"

I looked down at my lap and blinked hard to keep tears from washing me away. Words can be the biggest gift of all, especially when they come as a surprise. Once before in my life I'd been given a gift of words, and it was one more summer camp memory.

The last day of camp arrived. Somehow I had endured the summer. I rose while my cabin mates were still asleep and very, very quietly packed my belongings. Then I left the cabin for the last time without looking back. I took my bag to the mess hall and put it on the porch. Unlike most of the girls there, I had not added any souvenirs to my belongings other than a single leaf pressed between the pages of a book. If anyone had stolen my bag I would not have cared, for I would never wear any of the clothing inside it again.

From the mess hall I doubled back to my tree, and climbed it for the last time. I went higher than I had ever gone before, and gazed out over the lake and beyond. The sun slid up into the sky, heralded by a changing palette of pinks and golds that melted into a sunny late summer day. I saw the buses arrive that would take us home again, and the cars of parents who were picking up their daughters. Below me girls ran back and forth, lining up for breakfast and then carrying their belongings to the parking area.

After a while the parade of girls thinned, and I was about to descend when I heard familiar voices coming along the path. Jodi was telling Kathy and Lisa about school and the fun she and her friends would have. She broke off and said, "Oh, pooh! I left my canteen in the bathroom after I filled it. Kathy, go get it for me."

"No," said Kathy.

"What?" The three of them stopped below my tree. This was my last opportunity to drop a boulder or a grand piano or something on them, but alas I did not have any large heavy items with me on the tree limb.

"No, I won't," Kathy said again. "You've been mean all summer, and pushed me around. I wish I had tried to be friends with Louisa instead of you, because she's always nice, even when you picked on her. I'm never doing anything you say again." And the little worm who had just turned flounced off to the bus, leaving Jodi and Lisa openmouthed. After a moment they went on. When the coast was clear I climbed down from my tree for the last time. I stood for a moment stroking its bark, thinking about how a few words can change everything. Then I went to the bus. I planned to sit by Kathy but another girl was already there, so I rode home next to a sunburned and freckled nine year old who swung her legs and chattered about her mother the whole trip.

Now I sat up straighter in my café chair. "I'd like to make one more toast," I announced, looking around the table. Everyone was listening. I took a deep breath.

"They say that a friend is someone who is there when you need them, and by that definition I have many friends at this table. Ambrose, for example, found me a place to stay when I needed one, ensuring that I will never ask him for another favor as long as I live."

Ambrose led the laughter.

"Earlene drives the biggest car and the hardest bargain of anyone in Willow County. Bob had to go all the way to California to find me a house. My cousin Kay—well, I can't even begin to say what Kay has done for me."

I reached over Emily Ann and locked my pinky with Kay's.

"But this toast is for someone else, someone who was there when I needed him. When I first met him I thought that he was more trouble than he was worth, but in the end he proved to be worth more in trouble than I could possibly have imagined." I paused and raised my glass. "Ladies and gentlemen and dogs, a toast to Rollo!"

All eyes turned to the terrier, who stood on the real Miss Mason's lap and looked around the table with his bright shoe-button eyes. "To Rollo!" rang out in several voices, and we drank in his honor.

Rollo barked.

THE END

About the author:

Sharon Henegar wrote and illustrated her first book at the age of nine. It was about wild horses. She had a long career as a children's librarian, and looks forward to just as many years as a writer. She has completed three books in the Willow Falls series, as well as *Shopping on Driveways: Advice for Thrifters from the Queen of Fifty Cents*. She is currently uncovering a plot involving a cat named Fig. She lives in Oregon with her storyteller husband, dogs Zoë and Edward, and cats Noll Baxter and Mrs. Wilberforce.

On Saturday mornings she pursues her avocation of thrifting in her green convertible. Follow her adventures as the Queen of Fifty Cents on her website (queenoffiftycents.blogspot.com).

Read the complete
Willow Falls series:
Sleeping Dogs Lie
In Dogs We Trust
The Dog Prince

And don't miss
Shopping on Driveways:
Advice for Thrifters from the
Queen of Fifty Cents

Order today from Amazon or
Saturday Books
www.SaturdayBooks.com

And watch for the next
Willow Falls Mystery,
coming soon!

www.ingramcontent.com/pod-product-compliance
Lightning Source LLC
Chambersburg PA
CBHW060532260626
47161CB00003B/874